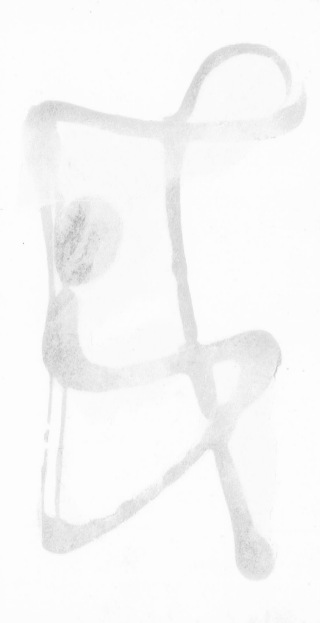

# Experiment in Terror

# Experiment in Terror

Bernal C. Payne, Jr.

Houghton Mifflin Company
Boston   1987

*Library of Congress Cataloging-in-Publication Data*

Payne, Bernal C.
  Experiment in terror.

  Summary: As his friends mysteriously disappear
one by one in the middle of the night, Steve finds
himself developing strange and terrifying powers.
  [1.  Science fiction.  2.  Extraterrestrial
beings — Fiction]  I.  Title.
PZ7.P294Ex  1987        [Fic]        87-17331
ISBN 0-395-44260-5

Printed in the United States of America

s  10  9  8  7  6  5  4  3  2  1

This book is for my sister, Mary Ann:
For all the night rides we went on, and all
the good talks we shared.

# Contents

# Prologue

*We drove out of town that night as fast as we could, trying not to attract attention, and I had this sick feeling inside my gut that I'd never see my family or my town again. But that was a lot better than never seeing Earth again. No matter what happened, I wasn't going to leave my planet with those creatures. No way. I'd go down fighting first.*

*I turned around in my seat and peered through the back window of the car and saw the lights of Summerville growing smaller; then I leaned back and gazed out the side window as we plunged into the total darkness of the country. First one farm slid by, then another, and the land became vast and flat and black.*

*I tried to pretend I was safe. Maybe I was. For a while, at least. I relaxed a little and glanced at the dashboard lights. We were doing over sixty. Then I looked at my girlfriend, Sharon, sitting behind the wheel of her mother's Volvo, eyes straight ahead, watching the headlights eating up the road. She didn't say anything and neither did I. The stereo radio was playing classical music, but I didn't bother changing the station. I didn't need any rock blasting away at me right now. This wasn't a joy ride we were taking. I was escaping from a nightmare of monsters. Only they were real and they were coming after me. I had to think. I needed to get everything that was happening straight in my head. I had to figure out my next move, because if I made any kind of mistake now, even the smallest miscalculation, it would be my last. On this planet, anyway.*

*I couldn't go back to town and risk falling into their hands again. I might not be so lucky the next time. I couldn't go to the next town and tell the police what was happening. They'd think I was crazy. And I wasn't ready yet to tell Sharon about it. How could I expect her to believe such an incredible story? I could hardly believe it myself. But it was happening, all right. They were back there looking for me. So where should I go? What should I do? Who was going to help me? It was too confusing. Too terrifying. All I could do was stare out the window and try to clear my head.*

*I couldn't think straight no matter how hard I tried. All I could do was remember the way things had been before this whole thing began. Back only a month earlier, to August, when my world was normal and happy and safe. Back before everything started changing . . .*

# 1
# The Group

It all started last summer when I turned sixteen. Or, I should say, on the day we all turned sixteen.

There are seven of us who were born on the same day, and we've grown up with each other over those sixteen years. We did everything together, starting from the time we were crawling around and fighting over each other's toys, to grade school, when we all sat together in class and played endless games of four-square on the playground during recess, then up to junior high and now when we were starting our junior year at Summerville High. All that time we were always going over to each other's houses, especially on the weekends. And we did a million things together over the summer. I guess you could say we're more than just friends. We're inseparable, like a molecule made up of seven atoms.

The people in our group are Jill Hawley and Scott Booth, Stephanie Dyer and David Voigt, Terry Reed and Roxann Powell, and me, Steve Taylor. And, just recently, a new member joined us: Sharon Baker, my girlfriend.

I'll always remember that Friday, August the tenth, the day of our birthday. It was a special birthday for us because we finally turned sixteen. The seven of us had spent the morning at the Motor Vehicle Department, taking the written and driving tests for our long-awaited driver's licenses. We came out of that experience exhil-

arated and a little shaken. Afterward, we went over to
Scott's to celebrate. Scott's parents weren't home, so we
had his huge house and swimming pool all to ourselves.
Well, almost to ourselves, what with the maid, Hatti,
keeping a sharp eye on us. But not sharp enough, because while we were inside changing our clothes, Scott
managed to permanently borrow a bottle of his parents'
French champagne. Then, in our bathing suits, the seven
of us sneaked into Judge Booth's library. It was a large
room with a high ceiling and stained-glass windows that
always cast a soft multicolored light over the mahogany
bookshelves and Oriental rugs and green leather chairs.

We held a towel over the bottle to deaden the sound
while Scott pulled the cork out with a muffled *pop*. Then
he filled our champagne glasses and passed them around.
He raised his glass, and his dark eyes became serious.
Scott cleared his throat, just the way his father, the judge,
always does when he has something important to say.

We looked at Scott expectantly.

"Here's to us," Scott began. "Sixteen years ago today
we were all lying next to each other in our cribs in the
maternity ward at St. Mary's Hospital, crying bloody
murder for our bottles. And here we are, sixteen years
later, toasting each other with a bottle of champagne.
We've come a long way together and, despite some things
I may have said to the contrary, I can honestly say I've
almost enjoyed every minute of it. You're the best friends
a guy could ever hope to have. So here's to us. May we
all be good friends forever."

We saluted, "To us!" and held our crystal glasses out,

touching them together with tiny chiming sounds; then some of us took our first sip of champagne and tried to act as though it was the most delicious thing we'd ever tasted.

Just then Hatti opened the door, took one look at us, and scolded, "Scott Booth! Shame on you! I'm gonna tell your folks what you kids are doin' in here and they're gonna be fit to be tied!"

Scott calmly raised his glass to the old black woman and showed her his perfect teeth. "And here's to Hatti, who wouldn't do anything to interfere with the calm and happiness of our peaceful home."

Hatti frowned at him and shook her finger. "You come outta this room right now and then I won't have to break up no happiness!"

"To Hatti," Scott said.

We raised our glasses to the flustered woman. "To Hatti!"

She gave us an indignant "Humph!" and slammed the library door behind her.

Not wanting to push old Hatti too far, we drank up and tossed the rest of the champagne down the kitchen sink and went out to the pool. Scott had good reason not to anger his parents that day because they were going to buy him a 1955 MG sports car for his birthday present. Scott had seen the car in St. Louis the week before and asked them for it. Well, I guess when you're rich, you're rich.

Over the years, certain people in our group had started going steady with each other. For example, Scott and Jill started liking each other when they were still in diapers. Back in kindergarten, they even used to hold hands. Now they played tennis and biked and jogged around the neighborhood together. They're the athletes of the group, always on some kind of new health kick. They plan to be doctors and someday get married and fill their house with kids.

I was stretched out at the side of the pool, soaking up the sun, when I saw Jill walk out of the patio door and sneak up behind Scott with a cold can of root beer in her hand. I could have warned him, but sometimes an inevitable act must be played out. Scott was sitting on the edge of the pool, dangling his legs in the water, when Jill put the can right up against his bare back.

"Ahhh!" Scott whipped around, then slowly stood up, scowling at Jill. "So, you want to play games, do you?" He walked toward her, hands outstretched, an evil gleam in his eyes.

Jill held her hand out to defend herself. "Scott! Don't you dare! I just put lotion on! Scott!" And just as he picked her up, she poured the ice cold soda all over him, laughing uncontrollably.

"Ahhh! Damn! Now you've really had it!" With that, he jumped into the water with Jill kicking and screaming in his arms.

While this silly business was going on, Terry and Roxann were diving off the high board, creating some nonsense of their own. Terry and Roxann have been going with each other since grade school. They're the clowns of our group. They know every joke, pull every

prank, and keep things going when they get dull. Right
now they were on the high board, singing out circus
music — "Dot-dot-da-da-da-da-dot-dot-da-da-da-da" —
while Roxann nimbly climbed up on Terry's back and
sat precariously on his shoulders.

"Laadieees aaand gentlemennn," Terry announced in
his ringmaster's voice to the audience below. "What you
are about to see will shock you. Never before has anyone
attempted this dive and lived. Watch carefully and be-
hold the magic of — the Amazing Flying Nerds!" And
they both broke out in stupid grins and fell butts first in
the water, giving us the finger all the way down. Splash!
Splash! Ha! Ha!

Now, David and Stephanie are a little different from
the rest of us. They're the most serious couple of our
group. They sat at the patio table playing chess under
the shade of a large umbrella, ignoring all the antics.
David and Steph are both accomplished musicians. He
plays the piano — jazz, classical, rock — and she plays
the violin, and they play duets all the time. But David
has another talent, too. He's developing into an excellent artist. Back in grade school, while the rest of us were
drawing people that looked something like lollipops with
teeth, David was sketching faces we could actually rec-
ognize. He's graduated to canvas and oils now, and his
paintings are just as good as some of the stuff I've seen
in the St. Louis Art Museum.

Which gets around to the last member of our group:
me — Steve Taylor. There's not much to tell about myself at this point in the story, except that I've lived a

relatively happy and uneventful life here in Summerville. Uneventful, that is, until the beginning of that summer.

I said before that there were seven of us. That was the original number. But that's changed, because now there are eight of us. I met a girl last June. Her name is Sharon Baker. Her family moved from the other side of town and bought the house just three doors down from mine. The moment I saw Sharon, something happened inside me. Call it love at first sight or whatever you want. All I know is that when I saw strangers moving in, I strolled nonchalantly over to the house while the van was being unloaded. Then Sharon came out the front door, and we took one look at each other, and the whole world suddenly came to a grinding halt. We just stood there — she at the door and me on the sidewalk — staring at each other for a few awkward, heart-pounding moments. Then she smiled and headed for me, and I headed for her, and we've been in love ever since.

Sharon was welcomed into our group the moment I introduced her to the others. Which was really something since none of us had ever considered letting any outsiders in. But Sharon was different. It was as if we knew she belonged with us right from the start.

Sharon didn't come with us that Friday morning to the license bureau because she and her two younger sisters had to do some housework while her mom went shopping. She was going to get her license in six days, when she turned sixteen. She was supposed to show up at Scott's at one o'clock, and I'd just glanced at my watch when I spotted her coming our way. She gave us a little wave with her towel. "Hi, Steve. Hi, everybody."

She was wearing a white wraparound skirt and matching blouse over her bathing suit. She's almost as tall as I am — somewhere around 5'11" — and she has the kind of figure that turns heads. I'll admit I don't like the way some guys stare at her but, in a way, I'm also a little proud that they do. Her face is golden tan and beautiful, with large brown eyes that pull you in so you can't see anything else but them.

"Well," she said as she came over to the pool, "how did everything go this morning?" She leaned over and gave me a peck on the lips.

"Great," I replied. "There are now seven new dangerous teenagers on the road. And when you get your license, there'll be eight. Look out insurance rates, here we come."

"Hey," Terry called over. "Who are you calling dangerous? At least I drive with my eyes open."

Everyone came over to where we were sitting.

Terry said to Sharon, "You should have seen your cool, collected boyfriend here. I thought I was going to have to do his driving for him when that state trooper walked up. Old Steve looked scared to death, like he was going to be arrested or something."

"Very funny, Terry," I came back. "At least I remembered to use my turn signal when I pulled out onto the street. And I turned my steering wheel in the right direction when I parked on the hill on Elm."

"Big deal," he said. "There's one hill in the whole town. So how often am I going to park on a hill?"

"You should have seen Jill," Roxann said, sitting down beside Sharon. "She tried to parallel park three times. Can you feature that? I thought she was going to wave a white flag and surrender."

Everyone yucked it up over that, especially Jill.

"And how about me?" Scott put in. "There I am, driving Mrs. Hawley's new Oldsmobile, and Old Lady Winslow pulls out in front of me on Industrial in her big fat Cadillac. I was so shook I almost crashed and burned right there!"

After a few more exaggerated tales, David said, "Yeah, but at least we can say we finally made it. We can drive now. That means we just took a giant step into the adult world, boys and girls. And personally, I think it's been long overdue."

"Amen to that," Scott agreed.

"I guess things won't ever be the same anymore now that we can drive," Jill said a little thoughtfully. "It wasn't so long ago that we were racing each other up and down the street on our tricycles."

Roxann gave her an envious look. "And now you and Scott are going to be cruising around in his spiffy MG."

"Please!" Scott raised his hand with a pained expression. "One doesn't *cruise* around in a vintage MG, Rox. This isn't some old beat-up Dodge Charger I'm getting, you know."

"Then just what does one do in a classic '55 MG?" I asked, winking at the others.

Scott gazed off and smiled to himself dreamily. "Well, you sort of . . . pop and bounce along winding roads with the wind in your hair," he said slowly, making driving motions with his hands. "It's just so . . . I don't know . . . so terribly British."

Jill rolled her eyes. "Oh, brother. I don't know if I'll be able to live with him when he gets that car. He's getting preppier by the minute."

Scott got up and walked over to a patio table. "And, with this golf cap Jill got me, my preppiness will attain new heights." He donned his new tweed cap and assumed what he considered a preppy pose.

Then Sharon smiled around at all of us. "Hey," she said. I forgot to wish all of you a happy birthday. When's this big ceremony I've been hearing so much about?"

Scott said to her, "The ceremony isn't that big of a deal. It's very simple, but very discreet. And now that we're all here, shall we begin?" He got up and went into his house.

Our little birthday ceremony goes all the way back to the very first one. When the seven of us were born at St. Mary's Hospital on the same day, our mothers naturally became acquainted (especially since the hospital broke some kind of record in births that day), and a close friendship developed among our parents. The mothers started visiting each other's homes, discussing things like formulas and feeding schedules and baby clothes. Then our fathers became friends, too, and began getting together for weekend golf and the monthly poker games that have lasted over the years.

Our mothers thought it would be fun to have one big party for the seven of us to celebrate our first birthday.

And, of course, it was a good chance for them to get together to show us off in our cute little clothes. They enjoyed themselves so much that they had a second party for us the next year, and a third one after that, until it developed into a tradition. When we turned thirteen, our mothers felt a little hurt when the seven of us told them we wanted to have the parties by ourselves. So our parties continued, but we never invited our parents, or our brothers and sisters, or any outsiders to them. And even though everyone thought it was a little strange, we insisted on doing it that way.

Each year one mother would bake a cake with all of our names on it. When Sharon joined us this summer, we added her name to this year's cake, even though her birthday was a week away. It was Scott's turn this time to host our party. We all gave out a cheer when he came out through the patio door carrying one of Hatti's delicious chocolate cakes with eight candles burning on it. He grinned and started singing "Happy birthday to us" and we all joined in. Then he put the cake on a table and made a little speech for Sharon's benefit.

"This cake symbolizes the unity of our group. And for the first time a new name has been added."

We all looked at Sharon, who blushed right through her deep tan. I put my arm around her waist and gave her a little hug, I was so proud of her.

"Sharon," Scott continued, "the ceremony is this. Each of us blows out one candle and makes a wish for the others. We go in order, according to the time of day we were born. Steve is the big brother of our little group since he popped out at the ungodly hour of three A.M., so he goes first. Steve?"

I went up to the cake and looked at Sharon's name spelled out in icing beside the others. Then I bent down and silently wished that she would always be liked by my group of friends. I blew out one candle and stood up.

Scott said, "And now Stephanie." Then Steph bent down, concentrated for a second, and blew out a second candle.

"Terry, you're next. And don't stick your nose in the cake the way you did last year."

I had to smile at the expression on Sharon's face; she really hadn't expected any of this.

"Jill. You're up."

Sharon watched the proceedings with great interest, and I could see a look of admiration in her eyes.

"Dave's next."

This candle blowing was David's idea, and we kept it up because it was a nice gesture to continue. Much more meaningful than simply exchanging presents, we thought.

"Roxann?"

We never told anybody about this — not even our parents. We figured there are some things a group does that should be kept private.

"And now me," Scott finished. "Because I'm the baby of the family." He made his wish and blew out the seventh candle.

Then I took Sharon's hand and led her closer to the cake. "Now it's your turn."

She looked a little panicky. "I . . . I'm not sure I know what to wish for."

"Try wishing we all get rich," Terry suggested. "That's always been one of my favorites."

"No. I think I'll do something different." Sharon leaned over, thought for a moment, and blew out the eighth candle.

And with that we all applauded ourselves. Then Stephanie held out her hand to Sharon. "Well, that's it. Now you're one of us. Let me officially welcome you aboard."

All six shook Sharon's hand. But I kissed her cheek. Boyfriend's privilege. "Welcome to the group." I smiled at her.

Jill handed her the knife to do the honors.


I remember that day especially because it was the beginning of the change.

After we finished off the cake, we all jumped in the pool and started splashing around, swimming underwater and grabbing each other's legs and dunking people and, in general, just horsing around. Then we took turns diving off the high board.

I was climbing up the ladder, watching Stephanie above me swan dive into the pool, when I suddenly felt dizzy. I stopped and held on to the rungs so I wouldn't fall. Then, just as suddenly, the dizziness went away. I was startled for a second, but I decided it wasn't anything to bother about. I made it up to the diving board, walked out, jumped up and down a few times, and prepared to jump — when it hit me again. Only this time it was serious! My head started spinning and I began losing my balance and I heard Sharon yelling up at me from the pool. I felt myself going over and down, falling through space — falling in slow motion, as in a dream — and when I hit the water, the lights went out.

The next thing I knew I woke up on the grass, coughing up water through my mouth and nose. Sharon was shaking me awake. "Steve! Steve!"

I tried to move, but I hurt all over. I must have hit the water like a dead duck.

Sharon was bending over me, holding my face in her hands, and her voice sounded desperate. "Steve? Are you all right? Steve?"

I opened my eyes and saw everyone staring down at me, their faces filled with concern.

I heard Scott say, "Maybe we better get him over to St. Mary's."

I sat up with a jerk. "No! Don't do that!" Which made me cough some more.

"Oh, Steve!" Sharon held me in her arms. "I was so scared! I tried to warn you!"

Scott was looking me over. "Did you hurt yourself? Maybe you shouldn't move."

"No," I said. "I think I'll make it." I didn't know if I

should feel dumb, or lucky that I didn't break my neck.

Terry asked, "What happened up there? You looked like you fainted or something."

I shook my head. "I don't know. I got dizzy for some reason."

"Are you sure you didn't hurt yourself?" Sharon asked.

"I . . . I don't think so. Nothing serious, at least." I looked into her frightened face. "No. I'm fine. Really." I forced a smile. "Anybody want to dance?"

Which made Sharon choke out something between a laugh and a sob. "You big dope. You scared the hell out of me, you know that?" She held me even tighter. "You started falling over and — and I couldn't do anything about it and —"

"Hey. It's all right." I started to stand up, but it took Terry and Sharon to help me the rest of the way. "There. See? I'm good as new." Which was a lie because I felt like a skydiver who had forgotten to use his parachute.

"Do me a favor, will you?" Scott was a relieved bundle of nerves. "Stay on the low board from now on. You just aged me by ten years."

"Sorry." I glanced around at everyone and shrugged. "I can't figure out what happened." I looked over my shoulder toward the empty diving board, still confused.

Sharon helped me over to the patio table and I slumped into a chair. She said, "If you had landed the wrong way, you could have killed yourself."

"I know, I know," I said, wanting to end this whole · embarrassing incident. "But I didn't. So let's not worry about it, okay?"

She took the chair next to mine. "Okay," she agreed, but she still looked worried.

After a few minutes of recuperating with a Dr Pepper, I was back in the water with the others. My head felt fine, though my back hurt a little from the fall. But by four o'clock I was back to normal and everyone had forgotten about my little tumble. We played a game of water polo, and when we finished, it was getting late and time for all of us to think about heading home for dinner.

Sharon and I said goodbye to everyone and left. We walked down the hot sidewalk, keeping in the shade of the tall old trees lining the streets.

"How do you feel?" Sharon asked as offhandedly as she could.

"I'll live. But I won't be winning any Olympic diving medals this year." To change the subject, I asked, "What did you wish for when you blew out your candle?"

"I can't tell you that. It would be bad luck." Then she said, "You know, I'm really glad that I'm part of your group. I don't care what other people —" She cut herself off, but it was too late.

I looked at her. "What other people think?" I finished.

"Oh, it doesn't matter to me now."

"No. Go on. What were you going to say."

"Oh . . . it's just what kids say about your clique. That you're all a bunch of stuck-up rich intellectual snobs."

I had to laugh at that. "Rich? Hardly, except for Scott. Intellectual? Sure, we're smart. But since when is having brains a crime? Snobs? Well, do you think we're snobs?"

"No. You're not snobs. There's nothing wrong with a crowd wanting to run around together. It's just that I've never seen a group as close as yours. I know you grew up together and all that, but there's something else."

"Like what?"

"Well, it's hard to explain. It's just that . . . you're all so much alike."

Which is true. David, Stephanie, Scott, Roxann — all of us have a lot in common, all right. We all have the same color brown hair and brown eyes and dark complexions, and we're built the same, slim and tall, and in a way our faces have some similarities about them, too. Everyone — especially our parents — noticed how much we were alike as we got older. But there are some other things that bother them. We're probably the healthiest kids in Summerville. Maybe in all of Missouri. We've never been sick in our entire lives. Not even ordinary things like the flu or colds or even getting headaches. Our bodies are perfect. Maybe, I realized later, a little too perfect.

Our group shies away from talking about these likenesses, and I was starting to feel a little uneasy talking about them with Sharon, so I tried to laugh it off. "My mom's convinced that the seven of us have so much in common because of the way the sun spots were on the day we were born. My dad says it must have been the water that month."

"And what do you think it is?"

I shrugged defensively. "There are a lot of people who look like us. Take you, for instance. You've got brown hair and brown eyes and you're tall —"

"I know." She shook her head with a thoughtful expression. "But that's not it. It's not just looks. It's . . ." Then she shrugged and smiled. "Oh well. It doesn't really matter. I like your group and that's what counts. And I like you, and that counts for even more."

But it would matter later on. And in a way none of us would ever have suspected.

# 2

# Breakfast and Other Important Matters

I remember how it was that Tuesday morning three weeks later, on the opening day of school. Everyone in our house was getting dressed, running here, dashing there, all in a hurry to get to the breakfast table on time.

It's not easy swinging from the carefree days of summer to the regimental routine of school. I set my alarm extra early so that I could take a shower without being rushed. I was almost through when my twelve-year-old sister, Ivy, started banging on the bathroom door.

"Whoever's in there, hurry up! My bladder runneth over!"

Ivy (short for Irene) was just as nervous about starting her first day of school as I was. Whenever she gets overexcited, she goes to the bathroom a lot.

"Use a milk bottle!" I suggested through the closed door.

"Steve! I'm your sister, not your brother! Now open up or I'll set the door on fire!" She pounded in desperation.

I opened the door and went back to shaving in front of the mirror. "Make it fast, will you? I still have to comb my hair and —"

"Out!" She grabbed my pajama top and nearly threw me through the door.

A minute later she came out, making a sarcastic face at me through her new braces. "It's all yours, fuzz face," she said, and stomped past me with exaggerated dignity.

"Thanks, tinsel teeth." I went back in to shave off the rest of the lather drying on my chin. By the time I finished combing my hair, my brother, Doug, was poking his head in the open door.

"How much longer, Steve?" he asked.

"It's all yours," I answered, putting the hair dryer and spray and other things away.

Doug's seventeen, a quiet sort of guy who never comes on strong and is easy to get along with. I can kid around with Ivy because she asks for it, but Doug isn't that way. A lot of things had been bothering him lately, and for the past few months he'd become a lot more serious than usual. Maybe morose is a better word for it.

I accidentally knocked Dad's English Leather into the sink, and it was a miracle the bottle didn't break.

Doug smiled at me. "Nervous?" he asked.

"Who, me?" I replied innocently. "Just because school's starting? Why should I be nervous?" Then I unscrewed the top of the aftershave and dropped it in the sink all over again. I scooped it up, slammed it down on the counter, and turned on the water to get the smell out of the sink. "I must be having a spaz attack." I gripped the bottle in a fist this time and patted some aftershave on my face.

Doug's smile fell a little. "I envy you. I wish I was starting my junior year over again."

"Oh, come on, Doug. You can't mean that. You're just —"

"Just joking," he said.

We passed each other, and he closed the bathroom door behind him.

But Doug wasn't joking. This was his senior year and he was greeting it with anything but enthusiasm. We all had high hopes that he'd turn his low grades around last year so that he could get himself ready for college, but it wasn't working out that way. Poor Doug. Nothing ever comes easy for him. He always has to spend twice as much time on his homework as I do and he still doesn't do any better than below average. I try to play it down, as if it were nothing, but I think Doug's given up. What's bothering him is that he doesn't know what he wants to do after high school. He feels the pressure more every day, as though time's running out on him. I keep telling him to take it easy, but I guess that's simple for me to say. I hated to see him down like this, but what could I do?

I finished dressing and went downstairs to the break-fast room, which is a screened-in porch just off the kitchen. My mom had it built as an incentive for all of us to eat breakfast together. She has this thing about all of us eating at the same time. She's always saying, "The family that eats together stays together." I know a lot of families who eat at different times and in different parts of their houses, even in front of a TV. But Mom would blow a fuse if we tried something like that. If one of us is late to the breakfast room or the dining room, every-one else has to wait for that person. With that kind of intimidation, no one's ever late, believe me.

I strolled into the kitchen. "Hi, Mom."

"Morning, Steve. Would you get the bowls out for me?"

I don't have any trouble with Mom's routine. I'm an early riser, so I'm usually the one who helps her set things up. Which is fine with me because that means I don't have to help clean up the mess afterward.

Mom teaches kindergarten over at Manchester Ele-mentary School on the other side of town. She runs the house with the same discipline she uses in her classroom. The clock on the wall in her class and the one in our kitchen tell the same time, if you know what I mean.

Mom glanced at me. "Excited about going back to school?"

I put on my casual face and shrugged. "A little, I guess. How about you?"

"Oh, you know me. Yesterday I regretted not doing all the things I'd planned over the summer, and today I'm anxious to get back."

"Yeah, I know what you mean. I sort of feel the same way."

Mom looked at me with that sad smile she sometimes gets. "Just think. You're a junior now. A big man on campus. And it seems like only yesterday you were —"

She stopped herself in midsentence, which meant I was spared some embarrassing remark about my being her little boy or something like that. I sometimes get mixed signals from Mom about my growing up. Well, maybe I'll be the same way when I become a parent. Who knows?

She took down some Wheaties and Corn Chex from the cupboard. "I bet Sharon's ready to get back to school."

Mom had had Sharon in her kindergarten class eleven years before. I guess that can go under the "Small world, isn't it?" category.

"Yeah. We're both looking forward to it." I glanced back at Mom. "All right, we're excited, we're excited already."

Mom sighed. "I wish Doug was just a little bit excited about school."

I put out the silverware and didn't say anything.

She continued, "I know Doug dreads this last year so. And that's really too bad. He should be enjoying himself during these golden years. They'll never come back. Never . . ."

As sometimes happens, Mom was talking to herself more than to me. I said as I put the milk on the table, "He just worries too much, that's all. He doesn't know how to roll with the punches."

"I know. If he could only relax and be more like —" She caught herself and went back to making toast. Then she asked, "Do you really think Doug's given up on the idea of college?"

I came to my brother's defense. "Mom, you know as well as I do that college isn't for everyone. Doug could be a bus driver or a plumber or a — I don't know. There are thousands of jobs that earn a good living and don't require a college education. Why, he could get a job working for the post office and make a heck of a lot more than any teacher could."

Mom nodded with a hint of teacher envy. "Don't I know it." Then she sighed again. "You're right. I guess I have to face facts. It's just that I had such —" She didn't finish her sentence. She didn't have to.

Just then, Ivy came bouncing in. "Hey. Are you sure school starts today? Maybe we made a mistake or something." She gave us a hopeful look.

"Dream on," I said. "Today's the big day."

"Well." She shrugged. "It was worth a try, anyway."

Mom went up to Ivy and beamed down at her. "Let's

see how you look." She nodded with approval at Ivy's new pink and white outfit. "Yes. You look just fine."

"I do not," Ivy moaned, hiding her pleasure at the compliment. "Every time I smile I look like a banjo. I think I'll wear a veil over my mouth at school. Maybe nobody'll notice my grillwork then."

Mom waved her hand with motherly assurance. "There'll be a hundred other kids wearing braces at school today, so don't feel like you're the only one. Anyway, if you don't act so self-conscious about it, no one will notice. Believe me."

I said to Ivy, "Listen. If anybody at school makes fun of you, you just tell them you've got a big brother who likes to throw junior high students into trees."

She eyed me with surprise. "Are you serious?"

"Darn right I'm serious. And if Doug won't do it, then I'll find somebody who will."

Ivy smirked at me. "Thanks, Steve. It's nice to have somebody like you I can depend on."

Just then Dad walked in, singing, "School days, school days, good old Golden Rule days. Reading and writing and 'rithmatic, taught to the tune of a hickory stick."

Ivy and I groaned and shook our heads.

"Ah, to be back in school again," Dad reminisced. "Yes, sir, those were the good old days."

Ivy sat down next to me and said, "Tell you what, Dad. You go to school for me and I'll take over the store for you. How does that sound?"

"Oh no you don't," he answered back, not doing a

very good job of hiding the tender nerve she hit. "You'll go to college and make something of yourself. Not be stuck in a store for the rest of your life like me."

As the story goes, Dad was getting ready to go to college after he graduated from high school. But his father had a stroke and died, and Dad had to take over his father's jewelry store to help his mother and two sisters get by. Dad turned it into the largest jewelry store in town and made a good living at it. But he always got a far-off look in his eye whenever he thought about that summer long ago when he didn't make it to college.

I said to my sister, "Look at it this way, Ivy. You only have ten more years of school ahead of you. Ten short years. A tiny decade. Big deal. It'll fly by before you know it." I snapped my fingers. "Just like that."

Ivy made a face. "Could we not talk about school for a few minutes? I think I'm losing my appetite."

"And just think," I went on. "An hour from now you'll be sitting in old Mr. Dewoody's math class, just like I used to, listening to him explaining the joys of algebra and not understanding a single word he's saying."

"Math!" Ivy pretended to gag. "Now you've done it! I think I'm going to toss my cookies. I wanna stay home!"

Mom chuckled at her. "You wouldn't stay home today for anything and you know it."

Just then, a voice from behind greeted us. "Morning everybody."

We all turned around to see Doug coming into the kitchen. He tried to smile, but it was worse than his not smiling at all. Mom and the rest of us greeted him back with a "Good morning" that was probably a little too cheerful. Then we all settled down to breakfast.

"Well." Dad opened up the conversation as he sprinkled out his Corn Chex. "This is going to be a big day for the two of you. Ivy's first day at the junior high and Doug's last year in high school. Quite a momentous occasion for the Taylor family, wouldn't you say?"

Mom gave Dad a warning glance, but he ignored her. Our eyes darted over to Doug and flicked back to our bowls. Dad waited for Doug to respond, but he just sat there pouring milk on his cereal with his eyes down. Then Ivy broke the silence by saying, "Maybe we should call the *Gazette* and have this historic event covered in the paper. They could take a closeup of me standing in front of school, smiling. The caption could read: 'Brace face grosses out everyone at Compton Junior High. School evacuated until further notice.' "

Dad rested his eyes on his daughter. "Ah, but there'll come a day when everyone in town will envy your smile. Trust me on that."

As usual, Dad said the right thing. And at that moment it hit me just how much I loved everyone in my family. It's like seeing the same tree in front of your house year after year, and one winter day when it's all lacy with snow, or covered with ice and sparkling like a giant chandelier in the sun, it suddenly strikes you just how beautiful that ordinary tree can really be.

And there I was, munching my Wheaties, looking at

each person sitting around me, seeing them as the great people they are. Dad, who gave up his own dreams and now dreams for us. Mom, who keeps us all together as a family. Ivy, my little sister, who isn't so little anymore and is turning into a young lady. And Doug, who is a great brother but worries about his future too much and keeps it all to himself. I felt lucky having these people as my family.

I was halfway through breakfast when Sharon walked up our side yard and came in through the porch door. She was wearing a khaki skirt, plaid blouse, and moccasins, and her chestnut hair was swept back at the sides the way I like it.

"Hi, everybody," she called out. She walked up to the breakfast table looking a little flushed and excited. She came up beside me, smiling with those big brown eyes of hers. "Hi, Steve."

I tried to be casual, but who was I kidding? When you're in love, it's as though the whole world knows, whether you try to hide it or not.

"Hi," I answered with my mouth full of cereal.

Dad said to her, "All ready for your first day at Summerville High?"

Sharon had been going to St. John's before she moved to our street, which is two blocks from Summerville High. After meeting me, she decided to switch schools.

Sharon said to my dad, "I hope I'm ready, Mr. Taylor. It's going to be quite a change for me, but I think I'll like it."

"Well, enjoy every minute of it," Mom put in. "Both of you." Then she included Doug, who was sitting silently across from her. "All three of you."

Doug looked up at Mom but didn't say anything.

Mom asked Sharon, "Would you like a piece of toast or some coffee?"

"Oh, no thanks, Mrs. Taylor. I've had breakfast."

"You sure? It's just sitting there."

"We have to go, Mom," I said, getting up. "I promised the gang we'd get to school early and — you know."

"Oh, I know. Check everything out. Well, that's what you're supposed to do. Go on. Blast off. Enjoy yourselves."

I grabbed my new Trapper folder. "Well, I'll see you all later."

"Show 'em your stuff, Sharon," Dad called after us as we headed for the door. "Just like Mary and I did when we went to old S.H."

I glanced back at my brother. "See you at school, Doug."

He raised his spoon to me. "Yeah. See you there, Steve. Want a lift?"

"No. Too nice out. We'll walk." Then, to Ivy: " 'Bye, foil fang. Enjoy school. Say hello to Mr. Dewoody for me. Tell him Steve Taylor sent you."

Ivy smirked. "Very funny. Then I'll flunk math for sure."

Sharon and I walked outside and started down the sidewalk, holding hands.

It was a beautiful morning, with the sun blazing away in a cloudless sky. Our street is filled with old sycamores, and their branches bend over on both sides of the street, touching each other, giving you the feeling of going down a long shady green tunnel. Dartmouth Street also has some of the oldest houses in town, though the house Sharon moved into is only fifty years old. Mine's over seventy. And there are a few century-old houses around. All of them are two or three stories tall, and quite a few have large porches with swings on them. A dozen sprinklers *swish-swished* on the spacious lawns of our neighborhood, and sometimes we had to dodge the water as we passed by.

I was saying, "Well, I guess this is it for summer vacation. It was fun while it lasted."

"It was more than just fun," Sharon said with a squeeze of my hand. "I met you, and that's the best thing that's ever happened to me."

I squeezed her hand back, smiling inside and out. "That goes for me, too."

"It does seem like summer flew by this year."

"I know. Now we both have two years of high school to look forward to."

"You make it sound like a prison sentence."

"Are you kidding? I'm looking forward to it. It's just hard giving up summer and all the free time we've had together."

"I know. But it won't be that bad. We can study together, you know. It's not as though I still live on the other side of town and go to St. John's."

"True." Then I asked, "How were your grades at St. John's — now that everything counts for getting us into college?"

"Straight A's. How about you?"

"The same. Remember? I'm the one your friends call a rich intellectual snob."

"I don't see much of my old friends anymore. Not since I met you. Anyway, as I said, I don't care what they say. Not anymore."

We walked a little farther, listening to our resident crows cawing to us from some tall oaks across the street. Then I interrupted my own thoughts by saying, "You told me once you want to be a nurse. I know it's a long way off, but where do you plan to go to college?"

"Well, my dad wants me to go to junior college here, then finish up at Washington U. in St. Louis. That's where he went. How about you? Where do you think you'll go?"

"I'm not really sure yet. But, as I told you before, I know I want to do something with designing jets or rockets. That's a dream I've always had. So, wherever I go, it has to be a school that's tops in aerospace engineering."

Sharon slowed down a bit. "Where do they have that sort of thing?"

"Well . . . actually, I was thinking of MIT."

"MIT? Where's that?"

"In Boston, or somewhere around there."

"That's pretty far away . . . isn't it." It was a statement, not a question.

Then I started thinking. "Yeah . . . I guess it is."

Then she stammered, "I guess that means . . . when we graduate . . . we'll . . . we won't . . ."

We took a few more steps in silence, and it hit me that this wasn't just kid stuff we were talking about. It was our futures! "Maybe — I mean — do you think there's a college somewhere that offers degrees in nursing *and* aerospace engineering?"

Sharon's eyes brightened. "You mean, the two of us go to the same school?"

"Sure. Why should we go to different schools? I don't want to leave you, you know that."

Her face bloomed into a beautiful smile. "I don't want to leave you either."

I suddenly felt all warm inside. "We'll talk to the counselor about helping us find a college. We'll look over some catalogues and talk about it. And when we make our decision, we'll tell our parents that's where we want to go."

"Oh, Steve, I'm really excited about this. Think of it. Both of us going off to college together."

I was excited, too. This was a whole new experience for me, making long-range plans like that. Especially with a girl I was in love with. There was a big world out there, and we were heading right for it. It was a little scary in a way, but being with Sharon was going to make it a pleasure.

Just then we heard a familiar car horn behind us. Scott pulled over in his gleaming white MG convertible, with Jill sitting beside him.

"Greetings, pedestrians," Scott called over as his wire wheels turned slowly at our walking pace.

"Hi, your Britishness," I answered back. "Must be nice popping and bouncing off to school in your own sports car." I drove his MG when he first got it and I'd give anything to own one.

Scott leaned back behind the wheel, grinning over at us. "Nothing like it, Steve. This is indeed the good life."

Then Jill said to Sharon, "If you don't mind getting your bones scrambled around on bumpy roads and getting bugs in your teeth on the highway. And you can forget about keeping your hair neat." She was wearing a scarf on her head a lot these days.

Scott ignored Jill's little gibe. "So long, peasants. See you up at school." His little car roared away, leaving a thin cloud of exhaust behind him.

"Next year," I vowed. "Next year I'm going to have my own car, I promise you that."

And then my brother and his girlfriend, Kim, drove by in his convertible. The top was down, and they waved and honked to us as they sailed by. Doug had worked for his car — a red 1966 Mustang, in flawless shape — and he was really proud of it. Sharon and I waved back and watched them round the corner onto Jackson, heading for the high school.

Sharon squeezed my hand when she saw the expression on my face. "Now don't get all hot and humid just because you don't have a car. Someday you'll have a new car and a nice house and everything you'll ever want."

I mumbled, "Yeah, I know. Everything I want." Then I slid my eyes over her way. "Does that . . . include you?"

She gave me a coy grin. "Is that some kind of proposal?"

"It could be."

"Well, either it is or it isn't. Maybes don't count."

My heart skipped a couple of beats. "Yes. Then I guess it is a proposal — postponed for a few years, of course."

"Then my answer is yes — postponed for a few years, of course."

I slowed down and looked at her in a state of mild shock. "Really?"

She grinned at me. "Of course."

We walked on, both of us in a state of euphoria at what had just happened between us.

Sharon put her arm around me and said, "I love you, Steve."

I brought my arm around her. "I love you, too."

Right at that moment, as we turned onto Jackson Avenue, I knew that our futures stretched out before us and we knew we wanted them to be together for the rest of our lives. It was the greatest feeling in the whole world.

But up ahead was our immediate future.

"There it is," Sharon said.

We looked up the street at the huge three-story brick building where we were going to spend the next two years of our lives.

We gripped hands a little tighter.

"Look out Summerville High," she said. "Here we come."

# 3
# Hints of Things to Come

It was good being back at school. There was an excitement in the air that everyone felt as students from all over town headed for the front of the school. I joined David and Stephanie and the others in our group as we stood by the front steps calling out to other kids we knew, making the usual first-day-of-school remarks, like: "Hey, John. They letting you back in?" or "How ya doin', Cindy? Like your lipstick." There was the usual joking and telling of what we did over the summer, and the gossip over who was going with who and who broke up over what. And there was always some juicy bit of scandal to pass around for everyone to enjoy.

Then it was time to go in, and the halls were flooded with a tide of noisy students. We saw the familiar faces of teachers we knew and elbowed each other when we spotted one we didn't know.

We headed for our classrooms, feeling a little superior toward the sophomores, wandering around like lost sheep, asking us where such-and-such a room or teacher was, and we big shots having all the answers.

As it turned out, I had a class with at least one person

from my group and two classes with Sharon; miraculously, all eight of us had the same lunch period. When lunch finally came, we huddled together at our usual cafeteria table, jabbering over our morning's adventures. We were all so hyped up, I don't think any of us ate much. And then, before we knew it, it was time for our next class, and everything started all over again.

By the end of the day I was thoroughly wiped out. I walked out of chemistry with Jill and Scott, the three of us carrying new chemistry texts along with our other books. Scott said to us, "Chemistry! Latin! American history! Biology! Is there no end?" He struck a tragic pose.

Jill placed a sympathetic hand on his shoulder. "Well, Scott, we can always drop out of school and be fruitpickers if you want."

He hefted all his books, looking down at them with an overwhelmed expression. "Is that a promise?"

Which was, of course, a joke, since both of them were top students and planned to be doctors.

"Hang in there, Scott," I said, putting my hand on his other shoulder. "I guarantee you that things are going to get a lot worse."

"Thanks, Steve," he replied with a heavy sigh. "I can always count on you for words of encouragement when I'm at my lowest ebb."

Terry and Roxann walked up to us in the crowded hall and suggested we all go over to her house for an after-school TGIT party (Thank Goodness It's Tuesday, naturally). The five of us strolled out and waited for the others. Sharon came up and slid her arm around my waist. I told her about the party and she was all for it. Stephanie and David walked up next and liked the idea of a party, too. We watched enviously as Scott and Jill jumped into their MG and roared off down the street. Then the rest of us headed over to Roxann's house on foot, talking all at once as we moved down Jackson Avenue.

I remember that after-school get-together of ours because it was the last one I'd ever enjoy as a normal human being.

Scott and Jill were waiting for us in front of Roxann's house. We all went inside and greeted Mrs. Powell, then went down to the rec room. The Powells did a fine job of fixing up their basement for entertaining. The place was done in knotty pine, complete with a pool table, Ping-Pong, a dart game, a bar, two old pinball machines, and an ancient jukebox. Sharon was still amazed by all the stuff down there, but for the rest of us, it was our home away from home.

Just for fun, we put on the jukebox, which is filled with the Powells' oldies but goodies: records like "Walking My Baby Back Home" and "Secret Love" and "Ghost Riders in the Sky." Mr. Powell has hundreds of them and firmly believes the old records are better than the new. Well, what can I say? We made buttered popcorn and broke open some sodas and picked up where we had left off, talking about the ordeal of our first day at school.

After a while, Sharon and I wanted to dance, so we punched a button on the juke, heard Elvis Presley start belting out "Jailhouse Rock," and started doing our imitation of a 1950s jitterbug while everyone stopped talking and jeered at us. Sharon and I did a pretty good job, considering we didn't know what we were doing. Then Terry and Roxann joined us, then Jill and Scott, and even Stephanie and David gave it a try. The place was really jumping, and we were all doing a super job of looking completely ridiculous — when it happened again.

I suddenly felt something buzzing inside my head. I was getting dizzy just as I had on the diving board on the afternoon of our birthday.

"What's wrong, Steve?" Sharon stopped dancing and watched me do a little stagger step over to the couch.

"Come on, Steve," Terry yelled out. "Don't give up so soon. Not when you're getting up steam." He was doing all sorts of fancy steps that the Powells had taught him.

I held up my hand and smiled weakly. "I give up!" I shouted over the blasting music. Sharon sat down next to me and I said to her, "Sorry. I think I just ran out of gas."

"You sure you're all right? You look kind of pale."

"Don't worry. It's nothing. I guess I'm just rock 'n' rolled out, that's all."

After a couple of minutes, the buzzing in my head went away and I felt normal again.

Sharon and I left a half hour later. We walked down

Elm and cut over to Dartmouth. The afternoon was hot and muggy, so we walked slowly in the shade. I kept wondering why I had had another dizzy spell. I remembered something about low blood sugar causing such things, and I started thinking that maybe I wasn't the perfect human specimen I'd always considered myself. When we reached Sharon's house, Mrs. Baker was working in her rose garden. She must have planted fifteen new rosebushes in the three months since she had moved.

When we came up behind her, Sharon sang out, "Hi, Mom!"

Mrs. Baker jerked around, startled. "Oh! You scared me! Sharon, you're always doing that to me! No wonder my hair is turning gray!"

"Sorry, Mom." She chuckled and bent down to give her a small hug. "I promise I'll buy you a new box of hair coloring when I get my allowance on Friday."

"Thanks, sweetheart," Mrs. Baker said. "Why don't you give all my secrets away." Then she smiled at her daughter. "Well, how do you like your new school?"

"Oh, Mom, it's really super. It's so much bigger than St. John's, and it has so many more kids. I'm going to like it there. I really am."

"Well, I'm glad. The important thing is that you like it. You can tell your father and me all about it at dinner."

I said to Mrs. Baker, "Your roses sure are blooming their hearts out, aren't they?"

"They sure are. I'm really proud of them. Here, Steve, smell this one. Tell me what you think of it."

I bent down and sniffed the coral rose. "Smells great. What's it called?"

"Tropicana. Here, why don't you take one home to your mother." She snipped a huge bloom off and handed it to me. "There. Tell Mary to put that on her dining room table and . . ."

I didn't hear the rest of what she said because the dizziness hit me again. This time I felt it coming over me. I got down quickly on one knee and pretended to smell another rose, and almost keeled over doing it.

"That's my favorite," Sharon said as she hunched down next to me. "It's called Snowfire because it's red on one side and white on the other." She leaned over and sniffed one while I was making all sorts of heroic efforts to appear normal. But it didn't work.

Sharon gave me a double take. "Steve, what is it?"

Mrs. Baker was eyeing me, too. "What's the matter?"

It was as if invisible hands were pressing down on my brain. Since I'd never been sick in my life, what I was going through really had me stumped. I'd never felt anything like it before. I closed my eyes, waiting, hoping it would go away.

I felt Sharon's hands on my back. "Steve? What's the matter? Are you getting dizzy again?"

I tried to shake my head, which made me almost topple over in the rose garden. "I . . . I'm okay. Just give me a second." I forced myself to stand up. I took in a couple of deep breaths and held on to Sharon's shoulder for support. "I don't know. Maybe I'd better sit down."

Sharon and her mom led me over to their front porch and sat me down on the swing. Just then, Sharon's two younger sisters and my sister, Ivy — all three around the same age — came up the walk, home from school.

I whispered to Sharon and Mrs. Baker, "Don't say anything to Ivy about this. I'm fine now. Really." I made myself sit up straight and attempted to act naturally as the girls came up to the porch carrying their new books. Ivy had found much-needed comradeship with her two new friends because they had just gotten braces, too. What's that old saying about misery loving company?

"Okay, girls," I said to the three of them, "let's see those million-dollar smiles of yours."

All three stretched their mouths wide and bared their braces and wiggled their heads at me in hideous metallic grins.

"Just remember what I told you, girls. Never smile during a lightning storm. And don't go kissing any boys with braces or you might wind up locking bumpers."

Ivy giggled. "That wouldn't be so bad if it was Tommy Rapaport."

The two sisters stuck their tongues out and held their stomachs. "Oh, yuck, Tommy Rapaport's a nerd," Cindy Baker announced to the world.

"I think he's a doll," Ivy countered, not in the least ruffled.

"Well," Mrs. Baker opened the front door. "It looks like everyone's back to normal, so I'm going in. Sharon, I need you and the girls to help me. 'Bye, Steve. 'Bye, Ivy." She went into the house.

Ivy looked at the closed door questioningly. "What did she mean by 'normal'?"

"I don't know," I quickly retorted. "That term shouldn't be used too lightly around you girls."

"My brother the comedian," Ivy fired back.

I stood up and tested my head. It felt fine. Then I said to Sharon, "I'll see you later. I think I'll flop in the air conditioning for a while. It's like an oven out here."

"Okay, Steve. I hope you feel —" She glanced at Ivy. "Well, see you later."

Ivy and I walked the short distance over to our house. My sister turned her eyes up at me. "You feeling all right, Steve?"

"Sure. Why?"

"I don't know. You look kind of funny."

"Thanks, kid. You look kind of funny yourself."

"I mean, your eyes look weird."

I guess she was right, because I started feeling that pressure on my brain again, and I barely made it up to my room.

# 4
# The Change

Knowing my mom and the way she frets over every little ache and pain Ivy and Doug and my dad get, I decided it would be better if I didn't say anything to her about this. Especially since I'd never been sick in my life (which worried her, too. You can't win with my mother).

We sat down to dinner at six and, naturally, the chief topic was about what our first day at school was like. I don't remember what anybody said because I was feeling that pressure on my brain again, only now it didn't make me as dizzy as before, but only came as a gentle pressure that wouldn't go away. I thought maybe I was having a headache, so I sneaked two aspirins out of the medicine cabinet after dinner and they seemed to work, because a while later the pressure went away. So I thought to myself, Big deal, you just had your first headache. So welcome to the human race.

To celebrate Ivy's first day at junior high, Dad said he'd take us all out for ice cream. I felt a whole lot better, so when Mom suggested we walk into town, I thought the idea sounded pretty good.

The temperature had gone down a bit as the sun began sinking over the rooftops of the houses across the street. A westerly breeze blew on us as we headed down Dartmouth, which made the two-block walk a little more bearable.

Mom and Dad walked ahead of us holding hands, which reminded me of that morning, when Sharon and I were holding hands on the way to school. It made me feel good inside, and I wondered if Sharon and I would have as good and loving a marriage as my parents did.

Doug seemed unusually preoccupied on our walk, and I remembered that he had been extra quiet at dinner. He had mumbled a few things about school, but that was it.

I said to him as we trailed behind the others, "What's up, Doug?"

He didn't say anything for a couple of seconds. Then he replied, "Oh . . . I don't know." Which is his way of saying that something's definitely up.

I ventured a little further. "Anything I can help with?" I hated to prod, but Doug can be so cryptic at times.

"No. Not really," he answered shortly, staring down at the sidewalk.

He can also be exasperating. "Then what in the world is it?" I insisted. "I'm your brother, for crying out loud. You can tell me."

Then he looked over at me with an almost angry expression on his face. "Steve . . . tell me. How does it feel to be so smart and know what you're doing and where you're going? Really. How does it feel?"

Now it was my turn to hesitate. Actually, I was floored by the question. It wasn't like my brother to say something like that. I couldn't tell if it was a question or an accusation. I lowered my voice. "Doug, I know you're shook up about this being your last year in school and all that, but really —"

Then he cut me off. "Forget it, Steve. Just . . . forget it. Sorry I said anything."

That really bothered me. I'd never seen Doug so edgy before. Well, what could I do? It was his problem and he was going to have to work it out for himself. If he wanted to confide in me, he knew I was willing to listen.

We walked into the downtown section of Summerville.

It was quiet, as usual, since most of the stores close by six. There was the old brick courthouse standing in the square of grass in the center of town. Running along its four sides are the four major streets that make up our business district. On Main — the street we were on — are Bradburn's department store, the Sunshine Shoe Store, and Marvin's Drugs (where Doug works on Saturdays), and next to that is Taylor's Jewelry, which belongs to my dad. A couple doors down from his place is the Greenleigh Ice Cream Parlor. Mr. Greenleigh has been making his own ice cream there since my mom and dad were kids and, as the story goes, that was where Dad proposed to my mom.

When you walk into Greenleigh's, it's a little like taking a trip into the past because the place hasn't changed much since it opened back during World War II. The floor is made of large black and white square tiles and the soda fountain is white marble. The tables have round marble tops and the chairs have small round seats, all supported on old-fashioned wire legs. Three ancient ceiling fans rotate slowly overhead, creating a delicious cool breeze of ice cream flavors which blow all over you. I knew the moment I stepped inside that a peppermint ice cream soda was the only thing that would save me from the heat.

"Hi, Charlie." Dad greeted old Mr. Greenleigh, who was smiling at us from behind the counter.

"Hi, Johnny," Mr. Greenleigh called back. "See you brought the brood with you. Hi, Mary. I keep feeding you ice cream and you stay as slim as ever. How are you, Ivy? Getting used to those new braces yet? Steve, you been growing again. Better cut that out. Doug, I saw you driving down the street with that girlfriend of yours, and she's as pretty as a picture."

We chatted with Mr. Greenleigh while he made our sundaes. Then we all sat down, talking about this and joking over that, just making sounds while the cold ice cream slid down our parched throats.

And then it happened.

Actually, two things happened at the same time.

Doug had been quiet while we were talking. Then, right in the middle of our conversation, he blurted out this bit of news: "I saw a recruiter today after school and . . . and I've decided to join the navy after I graduate."

All of us stopped talking and turned to Doug and stared at him. My mom and dad sat there, stunned, while Ivy's eyes flew open. Then everyone started talking at once.

What happened to me was entirely unrelated to what was going on at the table. Because I suddenly saw light shooting out from my family! It looked like a halo of colored light coming right out of their skin! My mom and dad and Ivy were radiating a bright green glow, while the light shooting out from Doug was yellow!

I couldn't believe what I was seeing! It was impossible!

I was sitting there holding a spoonful of peppermint ice cream up to my mouth when all this started to happen; then my fingers went limp, and the spoon fell out of my hand, clattering to the floor, leaving behind a slop of ice cream on the table in front of me.

Then the lights went away, and everyone around the table returned to normal.

It seemed as though I was coming out of a trance. I shook my head and looked around at everyone, slowly coming back to my senses. No one was paying any attention to me because they were all talking in loud voices to Doug.

"Don't do it, Doug!" Ivy was saying. "Don't leave us!"

My mom was doing her best to control herself. "Now, look, Doug, you've got all — Ivy, will you please be quiet! — you've got the whole school year ahead of you to think about this. You don't have to jump into a decision as drastic as this without at least giving it some serious thought."

Dad was saying, "The navy? Why would you want to join the navy? What's wrong with sticking around here? We have a good trade school right here in town if you don't want to go to college."

Doug didn't say anything. He just stared down at the table and withdrew into himself.

Then everyone fell silent. Dad glanced over at me and saw I'd dropped my spoon. "Aren't you going to clean that up?" he said.

I snapped to and started mopping up the mess with napkins. I picked my spoon up off the floor while mumbling an apology.

A few minutes later we walked out in the opposite mood from the one we'd felt when we came in. Mr. Greenleigh followed us with his inquisitive eyes. He knew something had happened and that he'd get it out of Dad in the morning.

The walk home was depressing and hot. We've made that walk I don't know how many times, but this was the first time that none of us said anything to one another. Everyone was thinking about Doug, and I'm sure Doug was thinking about himself; but what none of them knew was how much I was thinking about myself!

I couldn't understand what had happened to me. What had I seen? There was only one logical answer: I had simply seen some kind of hallucination. That had to be it. The news of Doug's wanting to join the navy must have — I don't know — shocked me or something.

To make myself stop thinking about it, I broke the long silence and said to Doug, "What made you decide to go into the navy?"

Doug sighed loudly enough for all of us to hear. "Aw, let's face it, Steve, I'm not cut out for college like you and Ivy. I'm not that smart and you know it. I don't know what I want to be. Can you understand that?"

I nodded. "Sure I can."

"I just need to get away, that's all. I want to go places. Get out of this little town and see what the rest of the world's like. I want to get on a ship and have some adventure, meet new people, see other countries." He looked at me almost angrily. "I've got to get away from here, Steve, or I'll go crazy!"

"Take it easy, Doug. I know how you feel."

"No you don't, Steve. And you never will."

I didn't say anything more because that strange sensation inside my head was happening again.

That night I had a hard time falling asleep. I kept thinking about that light I saw coming out of my family. What caused it? Was my mind going? Was I starting to see things that weren't there?

I tossed and turned for hours. Sometime after midnight I finally fell asleep.

And then I started dreaming about the snakes.

# 5
# Gargoyles

*We hit a bump in the road that jarred me out of my thoughts. We were still inside Mrs. Baker's Volvo and it was dark out, and I was still running away from them. My mind felt overloaded, with too many things happening too fast, and all I wanted to do at this point was go to sleep and wake up to find that all of this was just a bad dream. I glanced over at Sharon, sitting behind the wheel of her mother's car. She hadn't said anything to me in all this while; she just kept looking straight ahead out the windshield, driving in concentrated silence. I didn't say anything to her either, because I knew if I opened my mouth I'd tell her the whole incredible story and I didn't want to do that yet. Not while she was driving. I'd tell her when we*

*were far enough away and out of danger. Then all I could do
was hope that she believed me. She had to.*

*I was mixed up and scared, and all I wanted to do was
think about something else to get my mind off all this. So I tried
to relax again and gaze out the side window at the dark coun-
tryside rolling by. But my thoughts went back to that week when
I knew I had definitely changed. . .*

When my alarm went off that Friday morning, I woke up
feeling like new. Tuesday was a hundred years away,
and what occurred at the ice cream parlor seemed like a
strange dream.

I jumped out of bed feeling the excitement of Friday
and the weekend just ahead. After I finished dressing, I
went down and helped Mom set the breakfast table, and
pretty soon everybody came downstairs to eat. Mom and
Dad must have spent a lot of time talking over Doug's
idea of joining the navy, because they surprised us by
reluctantly agreeing that if that was what he wanted,
then it was all right with them.

I agreed, too, just to make Doug happy. But Ivy was
totally against it and said so to Doug in what was developing into a tirade until Dad cleared his throat and gave
her a stern look.

Sharon walked up to the porch, so I grabbed my things
and we took off for school on another beautiful morning.
I'd told her about Doug's little surprise right after it
happened, but I didn't say anything about my weird
experience with the lights. If my dizzy spells worried

her, then my seeing those lights would have turned her into a basket case. Anyway, I didn't feel dizzy anymore, and all I wanted to do was forget the whole thing.

We met the rest of our group in front of school and decided to see a movie at the Tivoli that night. There was a new horror movie called *The Gargoyles* that we wanted to see.

It seemed as though my classes flew by in a couple of hours. When the last bell rang, the halls turned into a mad dash for lockers and the front doors. I grabbed my books and joined the exodus, and that was about it for the day.

What happened that night was a little more interesting.

After I cleaned up and changed clothes and ate dinner, I walked over to Sharon's at seven o'clock and picked her up.

"I'm not so sure I want to see this movie," Sharon admitted as we started down the sidewalk. "Horror movies always give me the creeps."

I took her hand and squeezed it. "Don't worry. If anything comes out of the screen at you, I'll be there."

"Thanks a lot."

"It's only film and actors and red paint. That's all."

"Sometimes it's hard to remember that when something really gross happens."

"Well, if it gets too bad, you can always wait in the lobby with all the scared little kids."

Sharon threw her head back and let out a belly laugh.

"That'll be the day." Then she squinted at me with a daredevil gleam in her eye. "If you can take it, so can I."

"Atta girl. Look out monsters, here we come."

We turned the corner and had started down Elm Avenue when Sharon asked, "Steve, do you ever have weird dreams about monsters running after you? I used to have them all the time when I was a kid."

"All my dreams are weird. I've been having these dreams about snakes lately. Some really strange stuff."

"Snakes?" she repeated, making a face.

"Yeah. I think they were cobras. Giant ones. They were rearing up and staring at me and — " I had to smile. "I think one was even talking to me in some kind of foreign language. Bizarre, eh?"

"I'll say. I hate snakes. If I had a dream like that, I'd probably wake up screaming. A talking snake? Ugh!"

We walked down Elm a half block and picked up Terry and Roxann at Terry's house.

"I hope this movie scares the yell out of me," Terry said as we started back down the street. "I saw the previews and it looked totally awesome. These gargoyles were coming alive on the walls of this castle — ah! — and they crawled down on the ground and started creeping up on this girl — "

"All right, all right," Roxann interrupted. "You don't have to show off your twisted mind. We concede the fact that you're perverted."

Terry's face sagged into a hideous mask and his hands went up into claws. His voice turned deep and sounded like death. "And they came out of the walls and started crawling down toward the unsuspecting girl below!" He gave out a low, sinister "Heh-heh-heeehhh" for the desired effect.

Roxann sighed. "Five hundred eligible boys in Summerville and I had to wind up with Boris Karloff."

Terry put his arm around her waist. "You wouldn't have it any other way and you know it, Roxy baby."

Roxann looked back at Sharon. "Can you believe the conceit of this guy?"

We rearranged ourselves so that Roxann and Sharon walked together in front of Terry and me. I watched the two girls whispering and giggling to each other, and I was glad all over again that Sharon had been so well accepted by the group. It was almost as if we had been waiting all this time for her to come into our lives.

We stopped by Scott's house and picked up him and Jill. We seemed to have come along right in the middle of an argument.

"But a doctor in this town isn't going to make any money," Scott was saying as the two got out of their chairs on the porch, heading for us.

"Money isn't everything, you know!" Jill snapped back.

"Hey," Terry said to them. "What's this about money not being everything. It's the *only* thing!"

Scott walked up to us. "Oh, Jill wants us to stay here in Summerville and be small-town doctors. She has this noble vision of our running off on house calls in the middle of the night to deliver babies and getting paid with chickens."

"And," Jill put in with a scowl, "Scott wants to go to some big city and live in a penthouse and dine in French restaurants every night and make money hand over fist."

"You've got to be kidding," Roxann exclaimed. "Here you are, both just turned sixteen, and you're arguing over something that won't happen for years from now. I mean, really."

Scott turned to me. "Steve, I ask you. Would you stay here if you had a chance to work in a large modern hospital in a big city?"

Jill grumbled, "Big, big, big! Big deal!"

"Well," I began, trying to sound diplomatic as the six of us headed down the street, "you both have good points."

"Real good, Steve," Jill said. "That says a whole lot."

"All right," I said, "if you want to know what I think. If you go to college for ten years — or however long it takes to get an M.D. — then you have a right to decide how you want to use it. If you want to go for the big bucks, then — "

"Hold on!" Scott raised his hand in protest, walking backward, facing us. "It's not just the money. It's a chance to do some really important specialization in a large hospital. Even do some research. Experimenting. Work in a laboratory. St. Mary's is just a small potatoes hospital. It's hardly what I would call a Johns Hopkins."

Jill cut in. "Isn't helping people in your home town important, too?"

"Sure it's important," Scott fumed, "but it's not what

I want!" Then he calmed down. "Look, Jill, Roxann's right. We've got plenty of time to think this thing over." Jill settled down, too. "But I like it here in Summerville." Her dark eyes traveled around the street. "The old houses and the trees and the park and the people. I want to live where my folks live. And I don't want to leave my friends," she added, looking at us.

Then Roxann said, "I don't want you to leave either. Why can't we all stay together?" She threw her arms around Jill and whined, "Don't go, Jill. Don't leave me." Which was Roxann's theatrical and humorous way of saying something serious.

But Terry knew this wasn't the time to joke. "I still don't know what I want to be, but it's going to make a lot of money, I know that. If I can do it here in town, fine. If I can't, then I'll head for someplace else."

Then I said, "I have to agree. It would be nice to stay here where we grew up, but let's be realistic. The big money isn't here, and neither are the jobs. Some of us will stay here and some of us won't, and that's the way it is."

Roxann exclaimed, "But then we wouldn't be with each other anymore! Oh, bummer!"

Jill, a bit stunned, looked at Roxann and Sharon. "I don't want to even think about that. I don't want us to break up."

A temporary gloom fell over us as we crossed the street and headed up Sycamore.

"Hey, everybody," Terry suddenly said. "Come on.

What is this, a wake? It's Friday night. We're going to the movies. Remember? We can worry about our futures some other time."

He was right, of course, so we all lightened up and started enjoying ourselves again. Terry went back to telling us how a gargoyle in the movie carries off this teenage girl, and while she's kicking and screaming her head off, she starts turning into stone.

We picked up Stephanie and David on the last leg of our zigzag course toward town. When we walked up to David's house, we could hear a violin and piano playing together. As I said before, David and Stephanie were the artistic part of our group. They were also the most disciplined, both of them spending hours on their instruments, usually playing duets. And then David spent even more hours on his painting.

Terry, the clown, walked up to the front screen door and started beating on it. "Hey, in there! Cut that racket out or I'll call the cops!"

Then came the worst string screeching and off-key piano banging I'd ever heard.

"Okay," Terry yelled through the door. "That's more like it!"

David appeared at the door and said to Terry, "With your tin ear, I wouldn't doubt it."

Then Stephanie opened the door and the two came out.

We noticed that Stephanie and David were both wearing some rather curious grins. Roxann was the first to say something about it. "All right you two, what's up? You look like you know something we don't. What gives?"

Stephanie smiled at David, then turned to us, ready to split her seams. "Hold on to your hats, guys. David just sold his paintings to Mr. Skinner at the Tivoli! Isn't that fantastic!"

We stood there for a second in mild shock. Then I yelled, "You're kidding!" and slapped David on the back.

"How? When?" Terry wanted to know.

"About an hour ago," Stephanie told us. "Mr. Skinner called David an hour ago and said he had decided to buy them. They're hanging in the lobby now."

Sharon said to David, "You mean the ones you showed him last Saturday?"

"Yep," David replied with a sheepish grin. "All three of them."

"Seventy-five dollars apiece," Stephanie added proudly.

"Seventy-five?" Terry's mouth hung open. "You got two hundred and twenty-five dollars?" He gawked at David in awe. "You're rich! You son-of-a-gun! You're bucks up!"

Jill's eyes opened wide. "David! That's wonderful! That means you're a professional now!"

"I knew you'd do it someday, David, old man," Scott said. "And when you're rich and famous, we can all say that we knew David Voigt back when."

"Come on!" Jill said. "Let's get going! I can't wait to see them."

We nearly ran the three remaining blocks into town. We descended on the ticket window of the Tivoli, got our tickets, and rushed inside.

"There they are!" Stephanie said.

Sure enough, there were David's oil paintings on canvas, with the frames he made especially for them, hanging on the lobby wall. We congratulated him all over again and shook his hand and patted him on the back, and you could tell, underneath that shy grin of his he was really proud of himself.

We joined some other patrons who were already in the lobby admiring David's work. On the wall of the Tivoli they looked even better than when I first saw them leaning against the wall in his room. They were rustic scenes of our area: an old red barn and split rail fence on a snowy day; hills with a church in the background just after a storm; and the Mississippi River painted from the top of Sutter's Hill. Each one had a picture light on it, which made them look really professional.

Just then, Mr. Skinner walked up and announced to all his customers that David had done the paintings, and the small crowd looked at David as if he was a prodigy — which he is. We stood around in the lobby for another ten minutes until it was time for the movie to start.

We went inside and sat down, and pretty soon the place started filling up with people, most of whom we knew. Some of them came up and congratulated David, who was really basking in his new popularity.

Then the lights dimmed, and the movie started with a

closeup of a stone gargoyle at night staring grimly out from the stone wall of what looked like an old English castle. An organ began playing some pretty spooky music, and lightning flashed on the gargoyle's gruesome head. I scooted down in my seat, reached over to take Sharon's hand, and prepared to get scared out of my skull.

The movie got off to a slow start and nothing much was happening. But then came this scene of a teenage girl walking across the deserted castle at night, and she was just turning a corner when a stone claw came out of nowhere and swiped at her face. The girl grabbed her cheek and screamed, and then she looked up in horror as she saw a stone gargoyle on the wall suddenly leap down on top of her as the organ blasted a blood-curdling chord.

At that instant I felt my brain do something and I saw the audience around me suddenly light up in the dark! It was happening to me again! I jerked my head over at Sharon and what I saw paralyzed me: her face was a frightening, glowing red! I pivoted in my seat and saw a crowd of shining red faces!

"No!" I gasped. "No! No!"

Sharon swung toward me with a confused expression on her glowing face. "Steve? What is it?"

I was out of my seat, standing up, staring at the audience, unable to believe my eyes. The crowd looked as if they were on fire!

A man in back of me barked, "Hey, pal, wanna sit down? I can't see through you, you know." As I gaped down at him, he changed into a bright blue!

Sharon was tugging at me to sit down. "Steve, what's with you?"

I pulled my hand away from hers and ran up the aisle and pushed through the swinging double doors into the lobby. I stopped beside one of David's paintings, blinking at it blindly, trying to clear my head. Then Sharon came through the doors and ran up to me. Her entire body was giving off a purple light!

"Steve! What's wrong with you? Why are you acting like this? Then the light suddenly went out as though a switch had been turned off inside her, and what I was looking at now was a nice, normal, beautiful face — filled with confused concern. "What is it, Steve?"

I must have been as white as a sheet, with eyes as big as plates, because Sharon was beginning to look downright scared.

"Steve? Are you all right?" She took a couple of steps closer to me. "Steve?"

I managed a lame smile and pulled off the best acting job of my life. "Yeah. I'm all right. I . . . I must have dozed off for a second or something. All I know is I looked up and there was that monster on the screen. . ." I attempted an embarrassed snort. "So here I am in the lobby with all the scared little kids. Isn't that a laugh?"

Sharon took my hand gently. "You had me worried, you know that?"

I shrugged. "Yeah, well, I shook myself up, too. Sounds a little stupid, doesn't it?"

Then Roxann, who had been sitting beside Sharon, came into the lobby. "Hey. What gives?"

"Nothing," Sharon said immediately. "Nothing at all. We're just going back in."

Sharon and I started back for the double doors, Roxann gave us a bewildered look, and the three of us went back inside.

I sat through the rest of the picture, but I wasn't really watching it. I kept glancing around, waiting for the audience to light up again. And I knew if they did, I'd probably scream. I was scared. I knew now that something really serious had gone wrong inside my brain and that it wasn't going to go away. I also felt that whatever was happening to me was only the beginning.

The question was: the beginning of what?

# 6
# Trouble in the Park

It's not easy to explain what was happening to me. After all, I had a power I'd never heard of before.

I discovered I could "push" my mind out to people and see a colored halo coming from them. And what was really weird was that it came so naturally to me. It was as though I'd been able to do it all my life, only I hadn't known it. Maybe "pushing" isn't the exact word to describe it, but it'll have to do. Have you ever stared really hard at the back of someone's head and thought with all your might, trying to make them turn around and look at you? I've heard of other people doing it, but it never worked for me. Anyway, that's the closest thing to what I was doing.

That Saturday morning, while the five of us were eating breakfast, I pushed my mind out at Dad and saw a white light radiating all around him. I was prepared for it this time, so I didn't hit the panic button. I just sat there munching my Cheerios, watching my father glowing like a light bulb. Then I aimed my mind at Mom and — zap — she lit up white, too. Then I gave a bigger push and watched Mom, Dad, Ivy, and Doug all shining away in pure white auras. What I couldn't understand was why I was seeing people in different colors at different times. But that wasn't the question uppermost in my mind just then. What I wanted to know was why this was happening to me in the first place!

I didn't want to say anything about this to anyone, not even Doug. I don't know why. Something inside told me to keep it quiet. I was hoping that maybe it would go away — although I had a feeling it wouldn't.

"Steve? Is something the matter?"

I blinked myself back to reality and saw Mom staring across the breakfast table at me. "Huh? Oh, no, nothing's wrong. I was just thinking about something, that's all."

"Well," Dad said, "I want you to think about mowing

the lawn first thing this morning before the neighbors think we're growing a jungle out there. And, Ivy, I'd like you to pull a few weeds. Doug, how about if you tackle the garage tomorrow and clean some of that junk out." (Doug had a Saturday job at Marvin's Drugstore, so he did his work around the house on Sundays.) "As for me," Dad continued, "I think I'll paint the back porch tomorrow if it doesn't rain." Then he turned to Mom next and eyed her questioningly.

"Oh," she said, looking a little cornered, "you don't have to worry about me, John. I've got plenty to do, thank you."

I was thinking, while everyone was talking, that maybe I should go see Dr. Chase and have him check me over, because I was beginning to worry that what was happening to me could get worse. What could cause me to see lights like that? Maybe it was pressure on my brain that was causing it. What if I had a brain tumor or something?

"Steve," Mom said, "are you sure nothing's wrong? You have the strangest look on your face."

I straightened up in my chair. "I . . . I was just thinking about where Sharon and I could go tonight, that's all."

"Ah, love," Ivy sang out. "Sharon, I'm so in love with you. Please marry me. Please! I can't live without you."

I gave Ivy the evil eye. "Stick it, tin teeth."

She went on, undaunted. "Oh, Sharon, be my wife. Say yes. Yes!" She started kissing the air.

"All right, you two," Mom interrupted with a warning look. "Cool it."

Dad glanced down at his watch. "Nine o'clock. I'd say it's time for everyone to man their battle stations." He got up and said, "See you all later," and then he kissed Mom and left for the store.

We cleaned up the kitchen and went off to our individual jobs. I went out to the garage to get the lawn mower and was tugging to get it out from between the snow tires and the wheelbarrow when I scratched my arm on a rusty nail sticking out of the garage wall. "Ow!"

Ivy ran over to me. "What'd you do?"

"Oh, I stuck my arm on the stupid nail!"

We both looked down at my bleeding arm.

Ivy said, "You better put something on that fast. You don't want to get blood poisoning."

That gave me the excuse I was searching for to see Doc Chase. I showed my wound to Mom, mentioned the words "blood poisoning," and she called Doc while I washed my arm. Doc told Mom to send me right over since I've never gotten a tetanus booster, so off I went.

There was only one patient ahead of me when I walked into the old, two-story white house where Doc's office was, so I didn't have long to wait. Mrs. Day, his nurse, took me to one of the examination rooms and put something gooey on my wound. A minute later Dr. Chase walked in.

"How are you doing there, young man? Heard a rusty nail got you. Let's take a look at it."

Doc was getting on in years, but he still had that authoritative way about him that made me feel like a little kid whenever I talked to him.

"I guess I wasn't looking where I was going," I said as he took my arm and examined it.

"Well, that doesn't look so bad. I checked your record and it looks like you're overdue for a tetanus booster." He held up the needle he'd brought in with him. "This'll fix you up. Hold still."

I gritted my teeth, and the needle plunged into my arm like a hot knife.

"There, now," Doc said. "That wasn't so bad, was it?"

The heck it wasn't. But I forced a smile and said, "Naw, hardly felt it."

"That's funny," he said with a shrewd smile. "It always stings like fire whenever I get one."

I blushed, and there I was, a little kid all over again. "Well, maybe it hurt a little."

He jotted something down on my medical record. "Now then," he said when he finished, "anything else I can do for you? How about an appendectomy or a tonsillectomy? I'm running a special on moles this week."

I gathered up my nerve and swallowed. "Well . . . actually, I was wondering if you could check me over if you've got the time. You know, just to see if my parts are working all right."

Doc shot a glance at me. "Anything special I should be looking for?"

"No," I replied a little too quickly. "I feel fine."

"Just want a twenty-four-thousand-mile checkup, is that it?"

"If you wouldn't mind."

"No, I don't mind. That's why I'm here."

While Doc examined me, we made small talk about this and that, and all the while I wanted to tell him about my dizziness and the lights I was seeing. But I was afraid to because . . . well, just because. I asked Doc to take a look at my eyes, and he really got suspicious at that. But I had to know if he could find anything wrong.

"As usual, you're as healthy as a horse," he announced when he finished. "And now that I've said you're in perfect shape, why don't you tell me what's bothering you?" He waited.

How could I fool Doc? He's known me all my life. For one short moment I was on the verge of telling him everything, but I changed my mind. "Really, Doc," I said, having a difficult time looking him in the eye, "there isn't anything wrong."

I knew I looked guilty as all get-out, and I could see that he didn't believe me, but there wasn't anything else I could do.

We said goodbye and I walked outside, relieved that he didn't find anything wrong with me.

Which put me right back at square one.

I like being with my friends and all that, but there are times when you need to be on your own, so Sharon and I went over to Lewis Park and walked around by ourselves that Saturday evening.

There was a softball game over on the north side of the park, where the diamond and the stands are, and we could hear the crowd yelling and cheering in the distance. Some kids were riding their bikes, and a few old couples were out for a stroll. And, of course, an occasional jogger trotted by. Otherwise we had the park pretty much to ourselves. We were strolling by the pool —which was closed now — and we could smell the watery scent of chlorine in the humid air. We stopped and hooked our fingers on the chain fence around the pool, gazing out on the empty blue water.

"Steve?" Sharon's voice was low, as if she had something on her mind.

"Yeah?"

"I was thinking about what Jill and Roxann said last night. About wanting to stay here in Summerville after college. And then I thought about what you guys said. Especially what you said."

"And?"

She faced me, and I looked down into her beautiful deep brown eyes. "I guess what I want to say is . . . that I want to go where you go after we graduate from college. We don't have to live here in town if you don't want to."

"You know, I was thinking about that, too. Actually, we could have it both ways."

Sharon's thick eyebrows arched up. "We could?"

"Sure. I could work at McDonnell-Douglas aircraft in St. Louis, and we could live here. After all, St. Louis is only forty miles away. Driving time on the highway wouldn't be that bad, and — "

She threw her arms around my neck and kissed me on the cheek. "Oh, Steve, that's a great idea! Why didn't you say that before? Here I was, feeling so lousy about the whole thing."

I gave her a big hug back. "What do you mean, feeling lousy?"

"Oh, wanting to stay here. I don't really want to live away from my family, but I also don't want to stop you from doing what you want to do."

"Why should you feel lousy about that? And who said I wanted to live somewhere else?"

"You really wouldn't mind?"

"Of course not. Anyway, everyone I know lives here. And I'm not really crazy about living away from my parents, either. I'd like having a house here in town."

"Our house," she emphasized.

Her words made me tingle inside. "And we could invite our families over for barbecues in our back yard, and our kids could go to S.H., and . . . it would be a perfect life for us." I felt good all over just thinking about it. "And you could be a nurse at St. Mary's. That way, we could have it all."

Sharon's smile faded and her eyes became serious. "Oh, Steve, I love you so much. So much."

Suddenly, something went off inside my head. It was like a warning buzzer, an overwhelming feeling that danger lurked nearby.

A boy's sneering voice came from behind us.

"Well, well. Look who's here, guys. It's the paymaster, and today just happens to be payday. We came along just in time. Step right up and get your cash."

I wheeled around and saw Tom Norton and his two goons heading for us. My brain automatically pushed out, turning the three boys into huge brown lights. These jerks had been troublemakers all their lives. Norton had been kicked out of high school, and the other two had dropped out. And all three had had more than their share of run-ins with the police.

"Come on," Norton drawled, his open hand out in front of him — a hand that could turn into a fist at the blink of an eye. "How much you got on you, Taylor? You're gonna make a contribution to the cause, did you know that?"

Norton and the others stood in front of us while Sharon and I had the fence at our back. I looked around for help, but the park had suddenly become deserted, as though it knew Tom Norton and his idiot pals were on the loose.

"Come on! Give!" Norton slammed his hand into my chest, and I bounced off the fence with a clatter of metal. I saw Jim Parris pull out a switchblade. It sprang to life with a threatening click. I could take on Norton. Maybe two of them. But not all three. And not with that knife. I wasn't stupid.

"Cut it out!" Sharon yelled. "We're not bothering you! Leave us alone!"

"Shut up!" Norton yelled back, his finger pointing at her like a gun, a mean glare in his eyes. His voice dropped to a menacing growl. "Just shut up and don't make any noise or you're dead meat. Both of you. Get it?"

I got it, all right. I knew there wasn't any hope for us,

and I wasn't about to get Sharon hurt by not cooperating. These clowns were capable of anything. I took out my wallet. "All I've got is two bucks."

Norton snatched the two bills out of my hand. "Rich guy like you's got more'n that. Come on. Dig deeper. You've got five seconds."

"But that's all I've got," I insisted.

Before I knew it, he knocked the wallet out of my hand and held me by the shirt, pinned against the fence. "That's too bad, rich boy, 'cause now you're gonna pay with blood."

Another guy by the name of John Weatherford, who was even crazier than the others, grabbed Sharon and pushed her up against the fence. "I'll take her." He giggled insanely. "She's prettier."

I yelled out, "Don't touch her!" Without thinking, I shoved Norton away and put up my fists, ready to get my brains knocked out.

Just then something happened inside my head. Without my trying, my mind pushed out and did something that surprised even me. My mind commanded them to freeze.

And they did. They all froze like living statues.

One part of me couldn't believe what I'd just done while the other part instinctively knew all along that I had the power to do it. Out of the corner of my eye I saw Sharon turn to me, as if she couldn't understand what was happening. I had to do something quickly.

I said out loud to the three boys, "All right, I've had it with you guys. I played your little game long enough."

I yelled at Weatherford, "Take your hands off her now! *I said now!*"

What happened was incredible. Weatherford let go of Sharon, Norton didn't move, and all three just stood there with their hands dangling at their sides. They wore blank expressions and stared straight ahead.

I thought to myself, Jeez, it worked! I must have hypnotized them!

I glanced over at Sharon, who gawked back at me in astonishment.

I pushed out to the three guys and mentally ordered them to turn around and walk over to the ball field, and when they got over there to wake up — and never bother us again. After I gave them that mental command, I said out loud, "All right, I want you guys to get out of here." I kept my fists up. "No funny stuff. Just clear out. Get it?" And I snatched my two dollars out of Norton's limp hand.

It was a miracle. All three slowly turned around and shuffled off through the park like zombies out for a stroll.

Sharon grabbed my arm. "Steve! I can't believe it! How did you — What did you — I don't get it."

I picked up my wallet and dusted it off, feeling a little like Clint Eastwood on the outside and Woody Allen on the inside. "Come on. Let's get out of here," I managed to say without my voice shaking too much.

What happened was kind of funny when I look back on it now, turning Norton and his friends into vegetables, but at the time it had me even more confused than I already was. Because I seemed to have a second power to contend with, and I still hadn't figured out the first one.

# 7
# The Third Power

It didn't take long for me to figure out what the light coming from people meant. At first it was simply a trick: I pushed out and people lit up; it was as easy as turning on a table lamp. But after a while a pattern started to form. I discovered that different colors represented different emotions. For example, the red I saw in the Tivoli meant that everyone was feeling fear during the horror scene. The green light coming out of my mom and dad at the ice cream parlor stood for surprise or shock at Doug's news. Yellow was a little harder to unravel, but it turned out that it meant the person was depressed or sad. Blue was for anger. Purple for worry. Lavender for being happy. Brown, coming out of those three clowns at the park — and here I'm only guessing — stood for what someone feels when they're about to do something mean. I discovered people put out a gray light when they were sleeping. And when they weren't feeling any particular emotion at all, they lit up a pure white.

It took a week of experimenting — of pushing out and observing people — to sort this all out, matching colors with moods. Having that power didn't worry me as much as the second power, making people do what I commanded. That bothered me more. But I had no idea that something else was going to come along to make things even more confusing.

It happened at the end of the week, on Friday. I was in English, and my teacher, Mr. Aldridge, gave us the last fifteen minutes of class for quiet study. I was reading *Huckleberry Finn* — at the part where Huck is escaping from Pap's shack — when I heard Mr. Aldridge say, "If I ask Harriet out she'll refuse me, but I've got to try, be brave — no — yes! — I can't — but — Just do it. Go up to her and ask her to the movies, don't be a coward."

I looked up at Mr. Aldridge, wondering what in the world he was talking about. He was sitting at his desk, gazing out the window with his hands folded over his mouth. He was young and shy and a bit of a dreamer anyway, and it wasn't the first time I'd caught him staring off into space.

"What'll I do if she says no? Maybe she's going with somebody. I'll ask around. Maybe — ah, who cares — ask her out anyway."

Then I realized Mr. Aldridge wasn't talking to the class at all. He wasn't talking to anybody! He was thinking all this to himself! And I could hear his thoughts plain as day, right inside his head! I stared at him in complete astonishment. It dawned on me that my brain was pushing out to him, but I hadn't realized I was doing it. Then I purposely pushed out harder, looking straight at him, concentrating on his head.

Mr. Aldridge was daydreaming, and I was picking up

a jumble of words and thoughts and mental images —
like all daydreams. And seeing a purple light glowing
from him, I also knew he was worried about something.

What I "saw" in my head was what Mr. Aldridge was
seeing in his. He visualized himself walking down the
hall to a classroom. He went in, and there was the young
and pretty Miss Norris, the new French teacher. In his
daydream, Mr. Aldridge went up to her — and the image
went blank. Then it started all over again like an instant
replay. He walked up to her and said "Hi" — then the
picture went dead again. After a few more false starts, he
walked up to her once more and this time asked Miss
Harriet Norris if she would like to go to the show with
him this weekend. She politely refused. Mr. Aldridge
felt totally mortified. Then he gathered up his courage
and made another trial run. He marched right up to her,
asked her to go to the show with him, and this time she
said yes.

I watched Mr. Aldridge smile dreamily to himself as
he continued gazing out the window, conjuring up all
sorts of visions about Miss Norris and himself.

Then the bell rang, which made the two of us almost
jump out of our chairs.

"All right," Mr. Aldridge said out loud, his eyes snapping back into focus, as the class got up and headed for
the door. "Have a good weekend. Make sure you get to
Chapter Twenty by Monday."

As I passed his desk, I saw his eyes sort of glaze over
once more, not paying any attention to the students leaving or coming in. I knew he was off again in fantasyland,

wondering how he could master his shyness and ask Miss Norris out for a date.

I hustled up to the second floor for my last-hour chemistry class, sat down in my seat, and went into a kind of quiet hysteria. A third power! I thought, My God! What is this? Why is all this happening to me?

Jill and Scott greeted me as they took their seats next to mine. I gave them a quick hello, but I was too preoccupied to say anything more. All through class I didn't hear anything the teacher said. All I could do was sit there and try to control myself. There wasn't any doubt in my mind now. I was in trouble. Serious physical trouble. And I was starting to wonder what other changes were in store for me.

But what scared me most was that a new part of me was waking up inside my body, a part I didn't even know existed! It was as though there were two of me living side by side! Maybe I was becoming a Dr. Jekyll and Mr. Hyde. I don't know why I chose that comparison, but I did. And it made me worry about my changes even more.

After class, I went back down to Mr. Aldridge's room and waited outside in the hall to see if the vision I saw was really going to come true. After his students left, he came out wearing an anxious expression. He headed down the hall with an unsure step, and I trailed right behind. We made our way through a few hundred students who were noisily rushing for the front doors and a weekend of freedom. Finally, we both halted where I knew we would: in front of a classroom door with the name MS. H. NORRIS above it. I didn't have to read Mr.

Aldridge's mind to know what he was thinking. Just as he straightened his shoulders, took a deep breath, and started to walk through the doorway, a brilliant idea struck me. What the heck, I said to myself. As long as you've got the power, you may as well enjoy it.

I stood in front of the door, watching Mr. Aldridge hesitantly make his way around the desks toward Miss Norris, who was erasing her blackboard at the front of the room.

Mr. Aldridge cleared his throat and greeted her with an uncertain "Hi."

Miss Norris turned around and smiled. "Oh, hello, Mr. . . . Aldridge, isn't it?"

"Yes. Bill. Call me Bill," he offered, clearing his throat nervously.

"Bill," she repeated with a smile. "I'm Harriet. I've seen you at the faculty meetings, but I guess we never really had a chance to officially meet." She wiped the chalk dust from her right hand and held it out to him across her desk. Mr. Aldridge reached over and shook her hand a little awkwardly.

I pushed out and fed a command into her head and heard Miss Norris say, "You know, I was just thinking, Bill. We should get to know each other better. How would you like to go to the movies with me tomorrow night?"

Mr. Aldridge's mouth dropped open, and he looked as though he was going to keel over her desk in a dead faint.

I walked away and headed for the front doors feeling

pretty proud of myself, knowing I'd just given Mr. Aldridge an experience he'd never forget for the rest of his life.

But I had done it for another reason. I was testing my powers to see what I could do with them. Now that I look back on it, it was also a chance — maybe a need — to make something humorous out of a situation that was dead serious. A sort of whistling in the dark, if you know what I mean.

I spotted Sharon outside on the steps talking to Stephanie. I walked over to them, trying to appear natural after what had just happened.

Stephanie looked worried as she said, "Steve. I just found out that David went home after lunch."

I blinked at her for a second, because what she said wasn't registering. "What?"

She said it over again. Then it sank in. "David? Went home? Why?"

"That's just it," Stephanie said. "I don't know. He didn't tell me he was leaving. He seemed okay at lunch. He's never done anything like this before. Unless something happened at home."

"Well, why don't we stop by his house and see what's going on?" Sharon suggested. "It's on the way."

I really didn't want to go anywhere except home because I had enough to think about with my own problems. But David's leaving school without telling any of us — well, that wasn't like him at all.

I tried to join in the conversation as we walked down the hot, shady street, but I did a poor job of it. I knew

Sharon noticed how preoccupied I was, but she didn't say anything, which was just fine with me. The last thing I needed was somebody asking what was wrong with me. We rang the buzzer and David's mother answered the door. Stephanie and I have known Mrs. Voigt all our lives, and we could tell at once that she was disturbed about something when she opened the door.

Stephanie said, "Mrs. Voigt? What happened to David? Why did he leave school today?"

Mrs. Voigt shook her head, looking a little puzzled herself. "I don't know what's wrong with him. He just walked in, said he wasn't feeling well, and went up to his room."

"Can we see him?"

"He said he didn't want to see anybody. That he wanted to sleep for a while." She seemed mystified.

I said, "That's strange. David's never been sick in his life."

"I know." Mrs. Voigt frowned. "None of you have ever been sick." Her words hung in the air between us.

"But," Stephanie said, "David and I were supposed to go over to Scott's tonight for a barbecue. Did he say anything about going or not going?"

Mrs. Voigt shrugged. "I can go up and see how he feels. He should be awake by now."

She disappeared inside the house. When she came back down, she said, "He must still be asleep. He doesn't answer. His — " She gave us an apologetic smile. "His door's locked. I guess he really doesn't want to be disturbed."

We weren't fooling each other by acting as though that wasn't unusual. I've known David all my life and I didn't even know he had a key to his bedroom door.

Stephanie blinked a couple of times at David's mother. "Oh. "

"Look," Mrs. Voigt said, trying to brighten up. "I'll tell him you were here when he wakes up, and I'll have him call you. Okay?"

"Thanks, Mrs. Voigt. I . . . I hope David feels better when he gets up."

The woman tried to smile. "I'm sure he will. He's been painting up in his room so late at night recently. I guess he just finally wore himself out."

We said goodbye and headed back down the street. Sharon and I dropped Stephanie at her house and walked on.

Sharon said, "What's the big deal about David, anyway? You'd think it was abnormal for him to get sick just once."

"You're right. I guess we're making something out of nothing."

Sharon looked my way. "Steve?"

"Yeah?"

"What's the matter with you today?"

"What do you mean?"

"Well . . . you've been acting a little strange ever since school." She took my hand in hers. "Anything wrong?"

I knew she was going to ask that. I tried to look cheerful. "Naw. Everything's fine."

"You sure?"

"Sure I'm sure." I wanted to change the subject to something that was bothering me, something I had heard in class today that set me thinking. "You remember what Mr. Harari said to us in Psychology today? About the mind being a universe? Remember when he said that the mind is capable of almost anything? That if we used all of our brain, we wouldn't be the kind of people we are today? That we would be mental giants with extraordinary powers?"

"Sure, I remember. And I remember the look on your face when he said it, too."

I let that go. "I've been thinking about it, and . . . I wonder if there are people walking around who . . ."

"Go on."

"Whose brains are capable of functioning at a higher level than everyone else's. Only they don't know it. Like maybe sections of their brains that have been lying dormant suddenly start waking up, and they can suddenly do things other people can't do."

"You mean like being psychic? Seeing into the future and all that?"

"No. Like being able to read people's thoughts."

"You mean mind readers? Well, they can fool some of the people some of the time — "

"But what if somebody could actually know everything you're thinking?"

"Then I'd stay as far away from that person as I could. That's invasion of privacy!"

I didn't say anything more about it as I left Sharon at

her door. Her reaction made it clear that I could never tell her what was happening to me.

When I got to my house and walked in the front door, Mom was just coming down the stairs. "Oh, Steve. I just remembered you're having dinner over at Scott's house and — " She gave me a closer inspection. "Something wrong?"

There it was again. I guess there wasn't any hope of my concealing how I felt. "Not really. Just a long day, that's all. I'm going up to my room and crash. If anybody calls, tell them I'll call back later."

I flopped down on my bed and started thinking about the changes going on inside my head. I wondered why they were happening to me, of all people, and how many more powers I would develop before it was over. I wondered what I would do if they didn't stop. I also wondered what I would turn into if they didn't. But I didn't think about it for too long, because I was fast asleep before I knew it.

I started dreaming about those strange snakes again. There were two giant cobras, and they had reared up and were swaying back and forth on their tails, staring at me. They started hissing and flicking their long forked tongues at me. Then one of them started talking in a foreign language, and the other one joined in. They sounded urgent, as if they were doing everything they could to tell me something.

What really scared me was that I could almost understand what they were saying!

# 8
## The Nightmare Begins

It's hard to believe that I could have had all these things going on and then appear at a Friday night barbecue as though nothing was happening. But I did.

By the time Sharon and I got there, Jill and Scott were putting the paper plates and utensils on the patio table and had the barbecue pit smoking while Terry and Roxann were setting up the badminton net on the lawn.

"I'm starved!" I announced.

Jill yelled over, "We're all starved! We were wondering when you guys would show up!"

Everyone else was having Scott's regular hamburgers, but I like my custom-made ones better, so I brought one with me that I had fixed at home. Scott peered down at what I was unwrapping. "I suppose you're having your usual hamburger à la garbage."

"Hey," I replied indignantly, "don't badmouth my burger." I held up the raw meat stuffed with mushrooms and tomatoes and a hundred other things. "Now that's a hamburger."

"Now that's a mess," Sharon countered.

Roxann walked up, eyeing my culinary masterpiece. "You'd better put that thing on the fire before it wakes up, Steve. I saw a giant version of something just like that in a movie once, and it was eating Tokyo."

Scott leaned over toward it. "What's in that thing,

anyway? I think something's moving inside."

"Funny," I huffed. "I'm surrounded by comedians. But when you smell my world-famous burger cooking on the grill, you're all going to beg for a bite, and I'm telling you right now, you're all out of luck, because this baby's got my name on it."

Stephanie arrived just then, without David. She didn't look too happy. I asked, "How does David feel? Isn't he coming?"

"I don't know. He never called back. I called his house, but no one answered."

"Hmmm," Scott mused. "That does seem a little peculiar . . . doesn't it?"

Our eyes flicked over at Stephanie.

Jill quickly said, "Oh, it's no big deal."

No one said anything for a couple of seconds. The fact was that David had never been sick in his entire life, and he had never missed one of our get-togethers. So it was a big deal, and we all knew it.

"I'll try calling him," Scott said at last. He went inside, brought out his cordless telephone, and punched some buttons while we all watched. "Hello, Mr. Voigt?" he opened. "This is Scott. How's David doing? Does he feel any better?" He listened for a moment with a strange expression growing on his face. "Oh, really? Well, I don't know why he's not here yet. Sure. I'll tell him to call you when he arrives. Of course. Talk to you later." He put the phone down on the table.

We all waited.

"Mr. Voigt said his wife had picked him up at work because his car's getting fixed. And when they got back, David was gone. They figured he felt better and was coming over here." He smiled. "See? No sweat. He's on the way."

Stephanie looked relieved and said, "Good."

"Well, then," said Terry, "let's get the meat going. David should be here any second. I'm starving to death."

We put the burgers on the grill and popped open some sodas and listened to Terry tell some of his awful jokes while the smoky aroma of hickory and cooking meat made our mouths water.

Five minutes went by, then ten. Some of us started glancing over at the brick walk that led from the front to the back yard. Fifteen minutes later, our meat was hissing and just begging to be devoured.

Stephanie spoke for all of us: "I don't understand. What's keeping David?"

"I don't know," Scott replied. "Maybe he stopped at the store for something to bring over. He'll be here. Come on, everybody, let's dig in. I'm famished."

But by the time we were halfway through, we were all glancing over at the brick path, wondering when in the world David was going to show up. And when the last bite on our plates was gone, we had stopped talking. We looked at our watches.

"This is ridiculous." Scott picked up the phone again. "Hello, Mr. Voigt? This is Scott again. Did David change his mind? He's not here yet and — " He frowned. "I don't know," he said. "We thought maybe he went somewhere first, then would be coming over here." His eyes traveled over to Stephanie. "Yes. I'll have him call. Sure. So long." He looked at all of us and shrugged. "They don't know why he isn't here."

And neither did we. It was seven o'clock.

By seven-thirty we were genuinely worried. Scott went in and told his parents what was happening, and then there were nine of us who were worried.

Just before eight, David's father drove up the driveway and walked around to the back of the house. He took us all in with one glance and his face fell. "David hasn't shown up yet?" he asked.

Scott answered, "No, Mr. Voigt. I haven't heard a word from him."

Just then, Scott's mother and father came outside.

"Ted," Judge Booth greeted him, "what's this about David?"

"I don't know, Carl. He just disappeared on us." Mr. Voigt tried to act as though his son was playing some kind of practical joke, but his troubled eyes gave him away.

"I don't understand," Mrs. Booth said. "David wouldn't do something like this."

"I know." Mr. Voigt's brow wrinkled. "I'm . . . I'm beginning to think that something might have happened to him." He attempted a faint smile and failed.

There was a long tense moment when we all glanced at one another while the air grew heavier around us.

"Where's Martha?" Mrs. Booth asked.

"She's home . . . in case David calls."

None of us liked the sound of that, either.

"Why don't you sit down, Ted?" Judge Booth offered. "Let's try to think this thing out."

"No." Mr. Voigt shook his head. "I'm going to drive around. Maybe I'll see David on the street somewhere."

"Then I'll go with you," Judge Booth said, and both men left.

I've never experienced minutes that dragged by the way the next ones did. The sun was gone and the sky grew dark, and we started getting scared. Because the night is when all those little demons and hobgoblins inside you start waking up — what my sister used to call "bogeyman time." The air became hotter, and it closed in on us till I could hardly breathe. We were all sweating and nervous, and when the phone rang, we nearly jumped out of our skins.

Mrs. Booth answered it, talked for a few seconds, then hung up. "It was your father," she told Scott. "He and Mr. Voigt are at the police station. They . . . they haven't found David yet."

And they wouldn't. Because that was the night David Voigt disappeared.

None of us went home that night. All of our parents came over to Scott's house and sat around discussing the situation, and while the police were over at the Voigts' asking questions, the rest of us were racking our brains for answers to this mystery. A uniformed cop came over and asked us some questions about Dave, but we weren't any help.

Poor Stephanie was almost hysterical. When her parents came over, they tried to take her home, but she flatly refused to leave. She wanted to be with us. We made phone calls to every possible place David could have been at that time of night. Then we decided we couldn't just sit around any longer, so we broke up into three pairs and drove around town, searching everywhere. I took my mother's car, and Sharon and I explored Bugler's Market, the Tivoli, a couple of hamburger joints, and the drive-in — but no David. We cruised around downtown and the neighborhoods for a long time, but by midnight the town was closed up and asleep, so we headed back to Scott's. By three in the morning, we were all looking pretty bleary-eyed. All of our parents had gone home, and Scott's parents had gone to bed. That left the seven of us, confused and exhausted, sitting in Scott's den.

Stephanie was completely drained from crying so much. She just sat in a chair staring off at nothing, her eyes bloodshot and lifeless. We wanted to take her home, but we didn't press it because we knew she needed us more than ever and that being alone in her room could do her in for sure. Anyway, we all needed each other that long, terrible night.

It was so hard to believe that it was actually happening. Nothing out of the ordinary had ever happened to any of us before. And now that we had done everything we could think of, we just sat around, feeling helpless and worried and scared.

Jill broke the silence. "David didn't run away. We all know that."

We nodded in agreement. It was hard talking in front of Stephanie because we didn't want to upset her any more than she already was. She knew that, so she took it upon herself to say what we were all thinking: "There isn't any reason for David to run away. I would have known if there was a reason for it. We all would have. He couldn't have done something like that. He — " Her voice broke for a moment, and we thought she was going to start crying again. But she composed herself and went on. "If he didn't run away . . . then what's happened to him?"

We all looked at her, then down at the floor.

"He could have been kidnapped," Jill whispered, more to herself than to us.

"That's impossible," I objected. "In broad daylight? David? A sixteen-year-old boy kidnapped in broad daylight in Summerville? Come on now."

Roxann jumped up from her chair and started pacing. She was too full of coffee to sit still. "First of all," she said, "something like that has never happened in this town. I asked my parents when they were here. No one has ever been kidnapped in Summerville."

Sharon began, "But that doesn't mean it couldn't — " She stopped and glanced my way, then went back to staring at the floor.

"And in the second place," Roxann kept on, "David would never let himself get into that kind of a situation. He's not a little kid. Do you think some guy's going to pull up next to David and offer him a piece of candy and expect him to get into a strange car? I mean, come on!"

"Anyway," Scott said, "Dave's not exactly a weakling. He could handle himself if — "

"But," Stephanie cut in, "what if some crazy guy pulled a gun on David?"

Roxann waved a hand at her. "The third thing is, who would want to kidnap David? There are kids in this town with richer parents than his. Look at Scott, for instance. His parents are loaded. Why didn't they kidnap him?"

Scott went a little pale at that thought.

Roxann shook her head. "No. David wasn't kidnapped. Let's not even waste our time with that theory."

"So what's left?" Jill asked. "Murder? Come on, let's bring it out in the open. Why hide it? Do we think David was murdered?"

"No!" Terry shouted a little too loudly. He lowered his voice. "No way. Who would murder David? He was such a quiet, nice guy. He was the kind of person everybody liked."

We heard Terry speak of David in the past tense, and it almost sounded like an obituary.

I spoke up next. "David lives a block and a half from here. How could he be murdered in broad daylight walking on the sidewalk from there to here? And where's the body? The police have combed the area and so have we.

Nobody's reported seeing anything, and you know you can't stub your toe in this town without somebody seeing it happen."

"A crazy man," Stephanie moaned. "It could have been a — "

"In daylight?" I insisted.

We all fell silent once again.

"Amnesia!" Scott snapped his fingers. "Listen. David was sick. He's never been sick before in his life. Maybe he was coming down with something serious. Maybe he was burning up with fever in his room all that time, and when his mom left the house, he got up, delirious, and just wandered off. He could have gone down the street from his house and wandered into the park, out of his head with fever!"

We were on our feet in a second. Scott called the Voigts and told them his theory. Mr. Voigt relayed it to the police, who picked up on it immediately. They said that since it was only a few hours till daylight, they'd start their search then. But we didn't feel like waiting that long. We crammed ourselves into Judge Booth's Mercedes, stopped off at our houses for flashlights, and headed for Lewis Park.

We broke up into three search parties and began combing the park on foot, shining our lights everywhere, calling out until we were hoarse, walking until we were ready to drop. But we came up with nothing.

By five-thirty, we had had it. We'd been awake for almost twenty-four hours, and we were all emotionally and physically exhausted.

The police showed up with a few volunteers and dogs, and we decided to let them take over. Anyway, they were better at this sort of thing than we were.

Scott dropped Sharon and me off at her house and we got out, attempting to give Stephanie and the others a smile of encouragement. Then we watched them drive away, sick inside, wanting nothing more than to sleep and escape from this ordeal.

Sharon and I stood there on the sidewalk in the growing light of early morning, not knowing what to do or say. We slumped tiredly into each other's arms. Sharon spoke into my ear in what sounded like a defeated tone.

"Steve? Do you think David's dead?"

"I don't know. Back there, with Stephanie listening, I had to say I thought he was alive. But now . . . I just don't know."

Sharon gripped me tightly. "Oh, Steve," she whispered.

"Don't worry. It's going to be all right. You'll see."

Way down inside I knew it wouldn't be all right, and I think she did, too. And because we didn't believe it, we held on to each other even tighter.

Then I thought of all the crazy things that were happening to me and I wanted to tell Sharon about them, but I couldn't. Because what was happening to me was impossible, just like David's disappearing was impossible.

A little voice inside told me that more impossible things were down the road.

# 9
# Sergeant Coffee

I heard my mom's voice mixed up somewhere inside my snake dreams. The next thing I knew she was shaking me awake. I blinked up at her worried face and she said something to me.

"What?"

"I said there's a policeman downstairs who wants to talk to you about David."

I sat up in bed with a start. "David? Did they find him?"

"No. Not yet. They're still looking."

I hunched over, put my face in my hands, and moaned, "Then that's it. We'll never see him again. At least, not alive."

"Steve, don't talk like that. The police are looking for David everywhere. Even in St. Louis. Pretty soon the whole state will be searching for him."

"They're wasting their time. If he's anywhere, he's right here in town. I know it. I feel it!"

Mom looked as though she didn't want to argue the point. She knew how upset I was. "Well, anyway, you'd better hurry down. That policeman is waiting for you."

I looked over at my clock. It said 11:30, which meant I had had less than six hours of sleep. I felt wiped out. I threw on some clothes and tried to comb my hair, then splashed some water on my face and went downstairs.

The man sitting in the living room was around my dad's age but shorter, with wavy black hair, a square jaw, and deep creases in his face. He was wearing a summer suit, even though it was too hot out for one, and he definitely looked like a cop.

My mom said, "Steve, this is Detective Sergeant Coffee. He wants to talk to you about David."

The man stood up, smiled, and stuck out his hand. "Hi, Steve. Glad to meet you. Sorry I had to wake you up." His voice didn't go with his face. It had a friendly, easygoing Ozark accent to it.

I took his hand and felt the muscles in it. "That's all right. Glad to meet you." I sat down next to him and tried not to appear too self-conscious. After all, I'd never talked to a detective before in my life.

He got right down to business. "We still haven't located your friend David Voigt yet. I've been assigned to this case and I'm talking to David's friends — the people in your group — first. I've been getting some background information from your mother. She says the seven of you, including David, grew up together. Is that right?"

I nodded. "I've known David all my life."

"Then you and David Voigt are obviously close."

"About as close as two guys can get."

"Steve, I need to know everything you can tell me about David. Especially things that have been going on in his life recently. I'd like you to tell me anything that might help us find him. Can you do that for me?"

"Yes, sir. I'll tell you anything if it'll help."

So I started talking. I was rambling at first, trying to

find a direction. There just wasn't anything to tell, really. I told him things that David and our group had done
over the summer — the usual stuff — swimming, tennis,
bike riding, movies, get-togethers. I talked about our
first days at school right up till the last time I saw David,
at lunch period yesterday, and there wasn't anything unusual in the way he was acting then. It sounded so ordinary and boring as I went on. David was the most
serious of the seven of us. His life was quiet, and he
spent most of his free time painting and playing the
piano. The only outstanding thing that had happened to
him recently was when he sold his paintings to the Tivoli
Theater.

"I saw them," Sergeant Coffee said. "They're good.
Real good. Boy's got real talent."

"That's what doesn't make sense about his taking off
like this," I insisted. "He had so much to look forward
to. His painting was starting to pay off. Things couldn't
have been better for him."

Sergeant Coffee nodded slowly. "I know. It doesn't
make too much sense at all from what I've gathered. If
it's the case that he ran away," he added pointedly. He
looked over at Mom. "Mrs. Taylor, would you mind if
your son and I went for a little walk? I've been sitting
down all morning and I need a stretch."

"Why no, of course not," Mom answered.

Sergeant Coffee and I went out on the sidewalk and
started slowly down the street.

"It wasn't another girl," I said before he asked the
question.

Sergeant Coffee grinned at me with mild surprise. "I was warned that you're a sharp bunch of kids." He went on. "Okay, let's talk about girls. David wasn't going with anybody other than Stephanie Dyer, was he?"

I had to laugh. "David has been in love with Steph for as long as they've been alive. If there was another girl, we would have known it, you can believe that. Anyway, David wouldn't have disappeared over some girl. He isn't an idiot."

Sergeant Coffee gave me a sharp look with his professional policeman's eye. "What do you think happened to him?"

I shrugged. "Running away is out. Kidnapping's out. Murder's out. Pulling a prank's out. And I guess his getting a fever and wandering off is out, too. I don't know. I just can't figure it out."

"There isn't anybody — just one kid — who has it in for David?"

I shook my head. "You have to know David. He's the kind of guy everybody likes. He hasn't got an enemy in the world."

"Maybe none that you know of."

I shot a glance at him, but he didn't seem to mind.

"One other question. Did David use drugs? Be honest now. It could mean his life."

"I will be honest. David and the rest of us vowed long ago that we'd never use dope. We never have and never will."

"I'm going to take your word on that, Steve. I'm going to believe everything you say — until I find out different." He gave me a serious look that had the slightest edge of humor around it.

I nodded back. "That's fair enough."

Sergeant Coffee and I had gone around the block, and we stopped in front of my house.

"Look," he said, "if you hear of anything or think of anything, here's my card. Call me day or night." He sighed while slowly shaking his head. "This one has me stumped, Steve. I'm going to need all the help I can get. I'm going to talk to the others in your group. I'd appreciate it if you didn't talk to them until I've seen them all. Would you do that for me?"

"Yes, sir. I can do that."

"Great." He shook his head again. "I sure hope we get some good news soon."

"So do I. The thought of David being gone like this —" My voice trailed off as my throat tightened.

Sergeant Coffee nodded understandingly. "See you, Steve." He turned, and I watched him walk down to Sharon's house.

I decided to go over to David's and talk to his parents.

"Steve." Mrs. Voigt looked as though she'd really gone through the wringer. Her eyes were bloodshot and had dark circles around them, her face was pale and haggard, and her hair — usually perfect — was a mess.

"I just thought I'd drop by to . . . to see how you are."

"Thank you, Steve. Please, come in."

The living room was a wreck, with papers scattered

everywhere, ashtrays full, glasses and cups lying around. You could tell things weren't right.

Mrs. Voigt said, "My husband's upstairs taking a nap. He hasn't had any sleep. The police left an hour ago. None of us have slept. We —" She stopped herself. Then she nodded toward a middle-age woman sitting on the couch. "This is my sister, Ellen Frawley." The woman only gave me a tired nod and turned back to her magazine.

"Heard anything yet?" I asked.

"No. Nothing. The police have begun a statewide search. I know they're doing everything they can."

Her voice sounded weak and lacked conviction. I'd never seen Mrs. Voigt like this and it scared me, because she looked like a mother who would never see her son alive again.

I put as much confidence into my voice as I could. "They'll find David. He'll turn up somehow. I know he will."

"They have to." Mrs. Voigt's voice trembled. "He's all . . . all I've got." She wiped her red eyes with her handkerchief.

Before our emotions could get away from us, I quickly said, "Isn't there anything in David's room that could give us a clue?"

"The police already went through his room. They couldn't find anything."

I hesitated a moment. "Would it be all right if I took a look?"

Mrs. Voigt shrugged. "Well . . . I guess it wouldn't hurt."

I followed her upstairs into David's room. It looked the way it always did: littered with paintings, pen-and-ink sketches, water colors, tubes of paint, brushes, sketch pads, colored pencils, and an easel. It had everything except David in it.

I didn't know what I expected to find. I spotted his latest work resting on the easel: a half-finished oil painting of the pond in Lewis Park. It was first-rate.

"The police didn't find anything that would help?" I asked.

"Nothing. All his clothes are here. His money is still in his top drawer. We checked with the bank. The money he got for his paintings is still there, too."

"No letters? He didn't write down anything?"

"There was a sketch in his pad there on the dresser that the police took."

"What sketch? A drawing of what?"

"Oh . . . it wasn't anything."

I heard Mr. Voigt call out his wife's name from the bedroom across the hall. She went out of the room, and the second she left I tore off the next sheet of plain white paper from the sketch pad, rolled it up, and stuffed it under my shirt. I didn't like the way she acted when I asked about the drawing. It was almost as if she was hiding something. She came back in the room looking a little worse, if that was possible. "It's Ted. He's so upset by this. I have to go to him. You don't mind seeing yourself out, do you, Steve?"

"No. Of course not." I stepped out into the hall. I looked directly at the woman I'd known for sixteen years. "David'll turn up, Mrs. Voigt. He'll be all right. I know he will. There's got to be a logical explanation for all this."

She put her hand over her mouth, turned around, and walked quickly into her bedroom and closed the door. I had never felt so alone as I did at that moment, looking into David's empty room, knowing he was gone.

It seemed like an awfully long walk back home.

I went up to my room and took out the sheet of blank paper. I wanted to know what David had been drawing that made the police so interested and why Mrs. Voigt acted so strangely when she mentioned it. I carefully unrolled the paper and laid it out on my desk and stared down at it. I could see the lines indented in the paper when David had pressed down on the top sheet with his pen. I took a pencil and began rubbing the side of the lead back and forth lightly over the paper — something I'd seen done in a detective movie once. Impressions began to appear on the paper, and in a few seconds an image began to stand out. It was David's sketch of a cobra-like snake, reared up in an S-shaped curve. But, instead of its having a cobra's head, it had a head more like that of a human being. The upper half of its body widened out into a chest like a person's, with shoulders and arms and hands. And each hand had seven fingers on it.

Then it struck me! The snake dream I'd had just

before my mom woke me up a few hours ago! It hadn't been a simple cobra as in my other dreams; it had been a creature just like this one!

It couldn't be possible! How in the world did David know about the snakes *I'd* been dreaming about?

# 10
# The Lull Before the Storm

I had a lot to think about, but all it did was mix me up even more than I already was. I needed to tell somebody everything that was going on: about the strange things that were happening to me, about my dreams of monsters half human and half snake, and now about David's drawing of those same weird creatures. But who could I tell? My parents? Sharon? My friends? What good would that do? If I told them, they'd look at me as if I were some kind of nut. If I told Dr. Chase or Sergeant Coffee, they'd probably turn me over to government scientists for experimental purposes. No way. I wasn't about to have my life changed any more than it already was.

How, I kept asking myself, did David know about the snakes I was dreaming about? And why did he draw that picture just before he disappeared? It was too bizarre for me to handle.

I lay on my bed mulling over this mess until I couldn't take it anymore. I got up and went downstairs. The house was empty. Dad was at the store, Mom and Ivy were shopping, and Doug was at work. I didn't have anyone to talk to. I was scared for myself and I was scared about David, and it was driving me crazy!

I went for a long walk around my neighborhood to get my mind off things for a little while. Mr. McPherson was up on his ladder cleaning out his gutters. Mr. Manny was mowing his lawn. Mr. and Mrs. Wermeyer were planting a new pine tree in their yard. Mr. Tink was fertilizing his lawn. Linda and Martha Tibbits, both seven, were selling Kool-Aid out in front of their house. And the Hoffmans, an old couple who practically came with the town, were rocking on their porch, waving to anyone who passed by.

It amazed me how our normal, small-town life could go on like this when so many awful things were happening to me and my friends. For some reason, I expected everything to stop while we waited for David to come back. Oh, I'm sure everyone knew he was missing; but it was almost as though they didn't care. Life must go on, as they say. But it just didn't seem right.

I strolled over to Lewis Park and walked around for a while, and even stopped to watch a couple of innings of a softball game. Then I went up to the deserted high school and found myself thinking about my future and my life with Sharon.

Suddenly, I realized that I had joined all the other people in town who were doing a hundred ordinary things on an ordinary Saturday afternoon. Anyone seeing me walking around would never guess that my life was falling apart. But I kept on walking just the same. Getting away was just what I needed to clear my head.

For a little while, at least.

Because another tragedy was about to strike that night.


# 11
# The Storm


Mom fixed fried chicken, corn on the cob, and cherry pie for dinner; it was the first time I could eat anything since the news of David's disappearance. No one mentioned his name while we ate. I knew that was for my benefit and I was grateful.

In the middle of dinner, Dad said, "Doug, could you do me a big favor? I have a customer in Appleton who ordered a watch for his son's birthday. The watch came in today and his son's birthday's tomorrow. Could you deliver it to him for me? I'd really appreciate it."

"Sure," Doug replied. "I can run it over there after dinner."

"Thanks. I'll give you a couple of bucks for gas."

"You got yourself a deal." Then Doug asked me, "Want to go along, Steve?"

"Well, I was going to go over to Sharon's."

"Bring her along. I'll take Kim. We'll make it a ride. What the heck."

I knew this was Doug's way of helping me take my mind off David. Good old Doug.

Then Ivy asked, "Can I go along with you guys?"

But Mom put the fritz on that. "Ever hear of a fifth wheel? You stay here and help me clean up. Your time for riding around in cars will come soon enough."

Doug and I took off in his Mustang and picked up Kim and Sharon, then headed for Appleton, which was ten miles away. The radio had announced earlier that there was a chance of thunderstorms and, sure enough, a wall of clouds appeared on the horizon as we drove down the two-lane blacktop highway heading right for them. We pulled over, put the top up, and continued on.

I said to Doug, "Better step on it. Looks like a bad one coming up."

"Terrific," he sighed, and kicked it up to fifty-five. "Just what we need."

"Why don't we turn around?" Kim suggested. "You can take the watch there in the morning."

"Naw," Doug answered. "We'll make it if the storm doesn't come in too fast."

Sharon peered through the windshield from the back, where we sat. "I don't think we're going to make it."

We saw a distant flash of lightning ahead of us and, a few seconds later, heard a long *boom-boom-kaboom* of thunder rolling around in the darkening sky.

Doug said to Kim, "What's the address again?"

She glanced down at the slip of paper in her hand. "Thirty-four Clemons Avenue."

"I think I know where that is."

Another bolt of lightning stabbed the earth like a white-hot spear. The explosion sounded closer this time.

"We're not going to make it," Sharon repeated with a warning tone in her voice.

Doug grumbled, "Well, I'm not turning back now."

By the time we turned off the highway into the tiny town of Appleton, the sky was filling with low black clouds that swirled and boiled like an angry cauldron. The wind picked up, the temperature dropped, and the barometer inside me said we should have never left home.

We pulled up at the right address. Doug left the motor running as he jumped out with the package and ran up to the house. It seemed to take forever for the man to open his door. Then we had to wait while he took an even longer time writing out a check. In the meantime, the sky was going insane. I'd never seen clouds so low, so black, twisting around and around, shredding apart in wispy gray tatters as they spun faster and faster above us.

Just as Doug leaped off the man's porch and sprinted for the car, the street exploded as a bolt of lightning smashed into something a block away.

"Let's get out of here!" Doug slammed the car door closed and tore away as the first large drops of rain splattered against the windshield.

Kim looked anxious, then downright scared. "Doug, can't we park somewhere and wait this storm out?"

The windshield wipers started *slap-slapping* as more heavy drops pelted the car. The dashboard lights flicked on.

"I'll try to get ahead of it. Maybe we can outrun it."

We pulled back onto the highway, fishtailing, feeling the Mustang grabbing for traction on the wet pavement.

The world suddenly turned into midnight, as though a giant mouth had blown out the sun.

Sharon grabbed my arm. "I don't like this. I'm with Kim. Let's stop somewhere and —"

It was as if we were plunged into a black and raging sea. The rain came down in torrents, turning the windshield into a blind smear of cascading water. Lightning blasted the earth all around us with explosions of cannon fire. And the wind pushed our car, trying to throw it off the road. Doug pulled over to the side of the highway, turning on his emergency flashers. "We've had it," he said, and none of us liked the sound of his voice.

Then the hail came down in an avalanche. Chunks of ice pounded against the car, banging on the metal, cracking on the windshield, thudding on the cloth top. The plastic rear window collapsed inward, and we expected the top to go next, leaving us completely unprotected.

The next thing we knew, Kim was shouting, *"Oh my God! Oh my God! There! Up there! Look at that! We're going to be killed!"*

The three of us swung around to the right, where Kim's popping eyes were riveted, and our hearts stopped at once. Over there on the farmland, outlined by the constant flashes of lightning, the bottom dropped out of the swirling cloud, spinning, howling like an enraged monster. As we watched in horror, the monster began turning into an immense black snake, crawling out of the cloud, growing longer and longer until its tail touched the ground, alive and bent on destruction, twisting and writhing along the land about a quarter of a mile from us, demolishing everything in its path.

"Tornado! Get out of the car! Into the ditch! Quick!" As Doug threw his door open, a violent blast of wind hit the door, slamming it shut on his hand with a sickening crunch. Doug let out an agonizing scream, then forced the door open again with his other hand. "Out! Everybody out!" he yelled.

I scrambled out from the back on Doug's side and ran around to the other side of the car, where he held the door open, trying to get Kim out with his good hand.

"No!" she kept screaming over the howling wind. "No! I'm not going out there! Doug! Stop it! I don't want to get killed!"

Doug and I yanked the struggling girl out of the car, and I helped Sharon out of the back seat. As we did, another blast of wind tore the top off the car, and it sailed down the road like a demented ghost.

Then I saw something I couldn't believe. A speeding car was weaving down the highway, heading straight for us! I had just enough time to shout "Look out!" and I remember hearing someone scream as the car plowed into us.

A crash of thunder woke me up. Rain poured all over me. I was lying in the ditch, face down in the grass. I rolled over and felt a body next to me. It was Sharon and she was moaning.

"Sharon! Are you all right?"

"Steve . . . What . . . what . . . happened?"

I got up on my knees and looked down at her, scared out of my mind. "Sharon. Are you hurt? Tell me!"

"I . . . I don't know." She tried to sit up and moaned even louder at the effort.

I gave her a quick once-over. I didn't see anything serious except for some blood on her face from some cuts.

"What about the others?" she asked, looking around. Then she groaned and fell back on the grass.

"Wait here. Don't move. I'll get help." I staggered to my feet and spotted Kim, sprawled on the ground about thirty feet away. Her head was covered with blood. I had started for her when I noticed the Mustang and the other car in the ditch. The speeding car had run into the Mustang, and bounced off, and rolled over. It was smashed beyond recognition. Both cars lay there, twisted and ruined: the one car upside down, the Mustang braced on its side.

I looked closer at the Mustang through the pouring rain and screamed. I screamed again and ran up to it. Then I just stood there and went into shock.

It's funny, the things that go through your head in a situation like that. At that moment, I thought of the movie *The Wizard of Oz*, when the tornado picked up Dorothy's house, and how it flew through the air with all those weird things flying around it, like the old lady on the bicycle and the chicken coop and the trees and stuff. And how the house flew up into the land of the Munchkins, and how it landed, kerplunk, right on top of the Wicked Witch of the West. I remembered that scene clearly: how the witch's legs stuck out from underneath the house, and me, a little kid at the time, wondering in horrid fascination what she must have looked like under there.

I remembered all that because underneath the Mustang I saw Doug's legs sticking out — one shoe on, one shoe off — with the entire weight of his car on top of him. Only there weren't a bunch of little Munchkins, cheering over the death of the wicked witch; there was only me, screaming over the death of my brother.

"Doug! DOUG! DOOUUUUUGGG!!!"

I stood there helplessly, with the rain beating down on me and the thunder blasting in my ears, and all I could do was scream my brother's name over and over, wishing desperately that I could do something to save him. But I knew that was impossible. He was underneath a ton and a half of wreckage. It was too late. Nothing could save him. I kept thinking that he'd never be able to join the navy. He'd never see the world on that ship. And that he'd never have to worry about his future again because it had just come to a horrible end.

Just then something told me to push out.

Because I suddenly knew that I could lift the car with my mind.

I did push out — pushed out hard — giving it everything I had.

I saw the Mustang actually move an inch. Then another, and another. I mentally willed the car to roll back over on its wheels and I pushed even harder, feeling hundreds of pounds of metal rising into the air as the right side of the car slowly lifted off the ground. I gave one final push, and the Mustang rolled over in an upright position with a crash of broken glass and ruptured metal.

There was no time to wonder about what I'd done; I looked down to see Doug's mangled body pressed into the ground, crushed beyond recognition.

My head started reeling, and for a second I thought I was going to faint at the sight of that ghastly horror that had been my brother.

I stumbled up to Doug's body and stared at him while the rain beat down and the thunder exploded and the wind howled around us.

Then, a second time, something in my head told me to push out again.

I did. But in a slightly different way.

That's when I discovered that I had the ultimate power.

# 12
# The Fifth Power

It was as though I'd been submerged deep in cold dark water for a very long time until I slowly rose to the surface and woke up in an unfamiliar bed. It took me a few seconds to realize I was in a hospital room. My clothes were gone, and I had on one of those flimsy gowns that patients wear. I saw a young man in a gray suit walk in with a stethoscope around his neck. He came up to me and put his hand on my head. "Good to see you awake." The doctor smiled. "How do you feel?"

I licked my lips and tried to swallow, but my throat was too dry. "I — I guess I'm all right. I'm a little fuzzy, though. And thirsty."

He poured some water into a glass and put the straw to my lips. "Nothing hurts? Anywhere? You sure?"

"Yes. Really. I feel okay."

He had me move my arms and legs and head to see if everything was working. Then he said, "My name's Dr. Allen. You're in St. Mary's Hospital. We found your license in your wallet and called your parents. They're on their way now." He checked my eyes and ears with a light, then asked me who I was and where I lived and my phone number. I guess he was checking to see if I was thinking straight. I answered his questions, then the memory of the accident made me sit straight up in bed. "Doug! My brother! Where is he?"

I heard a familiar voice behind the curtain next to my bed. "I'm fine, Steve. The question is, how are you doing?"

I looked at the curtain pulled around the other bed. "Doug? Is that you?"

"Of course it's me," I heard him reply. "Who do you think it is?"

"Doug!" I jumped out of bed and was across the room in one step. I tore the curtain open, and there was my brother, smiling up at me in his bed. I threw my arms around him and babbled, "Then . . . then it wasn't a dream! You're here! You're really alive!"

"Of course I'm alive." He sat up, grinning at me. "What'd you think? It was you I was worried about. I woke up a couple of minutes ago and the doctor told me you were still out cold. Are you sure you're not hurt?"

"I'm fine. What about you?"

Doug looked himself over and smiled back up at me. "Good as new." Then he looked at his left hand for a second and frowned. "That's funny. I thought . . ." He flexed the hand a couple of times, then shook his head in confusion. "What happened back there, Steve? I remember we were standing by my car, but that's all I can remember."

"A car ran into us."

"Oh . . . yeah . . . a car . . ." He frowned, trying to remember. Then he said, "But, my hand." He held it up. "That's funny. I thought I smashed it in the car door." He looked me in the eye, frowning harder. "I don't get it."

Then a voice said, "Neither do we." I was suddenly aware of two men standing at the foot of Doug's bed. One was a doctor with a black mustache by the name of Bennett. And next to him stood Sheriff Richy — all three hundred pounds of him. Both men stared at us.

Dr. Bennett said to Doug, "Young man, you've really got us baffled. When you were brought in, you were unconscious and your clothes were ripped and dirty. In a number of places there were large holes in them. Jagged holes. And even though the rain washed most of it away, we found blood on your clothes." He ran his eyes over Doug, sitting up in his hospital gown. "But we can't find anything wrong with you. Not a scratch or bruise anywhere. Nothing."

He studied me next. "And the same goes for you, too. Both of you came out of that accident without a scrape." He gave us a very perplexed look. "I just don't understand it. Your clothes are ruined, but you're both unharmed."

Sheriff Richy said to Doug, "And I saw blood on your face, boy. Saw it plain as day when I showed up."

I had to say something to change the subject, and just then I remembered Sharon. "Doctor! There were two girls with us, Sharon and Kim! Are they all right? Where are they?"

Dr. Bennett said, "The one girl, Sharon, is in the room right across the hall. She's going to be all right. She —"

But I was already out the doorway, rushing across the hall in my bare feet. The same young doctor who had checked me was saying something to a nurse as they were leaving the other room. I spotted Sharon lying in bed with her eyes closed. I asked the doctor, "Can I go in? She's my girlfriend." But I didn't wait for his reply. I went in and walked up to the edge of the bed. Sharon had a piece of tape across her nose and a bandage on her chin, and one eye was swollen. Other than that, I couldn't see anything seriously wrong.

I took her hand. "Sharon. It's me. Steve. Can you hear me?"

Her eyes fluttered open, and for a moment they sort of wandered around the room in a daze. Then they fell on me with an expression of recognition. "Steve! You're all right! Oh, Steve, I was so scared!" She started to reach up for me and made a painful hiss through her teeth. Her eyes shut for a second, then reopened. "My arm. Oh, my arm . . ."

"It's not broken," the young doctor informed us as he came back in. "Just badly bruised." He smiled at Sharon. "You're lucky that's all it is."

Sharon reached up with her other hand and touched my face. Her lips started to tremble. "Oh, Steve, when I saw Doug under the car . . . Steve, I'm so sorry. Doug's dead, oh dear God, he's dead —"

"So who's dead?"

Sharon and I turned toward the voice at the doorway.

Sharon half gasped, half screamed, "Doug! You're — you're alive!" She gawked at him in complete astonishment. "But I saw you! Your car was — How could you —"

Doug walked up to her. "Dead? Are you kidding? I've never felt better in my life." He saw that the other bed in the room was empty. "Where's Kim? I thought she was in here with you."

Dr. Bennett's voice came from behind us. "I'm afraid she's in intensive care."

"What!" Doug spun around. "Intensive care! Why? What happened to her?"

"Hold on a minute and I'll check," Dr. Bennett said. "I didn't see her when she came in." He made a phone call that took only a few seconds. He gave Doug a "brace yourself" look as he said, "She's going to pull through. She's got a broken leg. The X-rays show a clean break. That's good. But she has a skull fracture. We have to wait and see how serious it is. She must have been standing next to the car when —"

"What?" Doug put an unsteady hand on his forehead while his eyes widened as he listened to all this. "Oh no. No! Kim has a skull fracture?" He looked at the doctor with pleading eyes. "Can I see her? Doc, can I see her for just a second? Please! I've just go to!"

"She's still unconscious," Dr. Bennett warned him.

"I don't care. I want to see her. Please!"

The doctor sighed. "I guess it'll be all right if you're quiet. But only for a minute. I'd better get you a robe first. Can't have you going around with your caboose hanging out like that."

Doug reached behind him and felt the open end of his gown. His face went from white to red. So did mine as I quickly sat down on the edge of Sharon's bed.

"Sorry," Dr. Bennett said. "I'm afraid that's one thing they haven't improved on in hospitals."

Doug backed out of the room, holding his gown closed, saying, "I'll see you guys later."

When he and Dr. Bennett left, Sharon gasped, "But, Steve! I saw Doug under his car! I saw his legs sticking out! He had to be dead! How can he be alive?"

I forced a reassuring smile. "You were seeing things, that's all. The shock of the accident and everything."

"No! Steve, I saw him! I did!"

"Then why is he running around the hospital with his rear end hanging out? Does he look dead to you?"

She gave me a blank look, shook her head slowly, and frowned. "I don't get it. I know what I saw. I was on the ground in the rain . . . and I remember rolling over . . . and there was Doug's car on its side . . . and I saw part of him sticking out!"

"It was your imagination," I said in a low voice, looking around to see if anyone was listening. "Just the shock from the accident, that's all. Let's forget about it for now."

She put her good arm around my neck and hugged me with what little strength she had. "Oh, Steve, you could have been killed. I'm so glad you're alive. I don't know what I'd do if I lost you."

"But I'm all right. Let's not worry about me — let's worry about you. How do you feel?"

"I hurt all over, and my arm's killing me. Other than that, I guess I'll live."

Just then the nurse came in. "You'll have to go back to your room now," she told me. I started to protest, then thought better of it. I didn't want to stretch the rules too far. So I squeezed Sharon's hand and backed out of the room with a silly grin, holding my gown closed behind me, which made Sharon smile a little. And that's what I wanted to see.

No sooner did I jump into my bed than I heard familiar voices coming down the hall.

"Steve!" my mother exclaimed as she rushed in the room. "Thank God you're all right!" She threw her arms around me and started hugging me. Then Ivy grabbed another piece of me and hugged that. Then Dad hugged me as well.

Things got even livelier, because Sharon's parents and her two sisters came in, then Kim's parents and all her brothers and sisters showed up. Then Dr. Bennett came back and talked to our parents, and Sheriff Richy was there to answer questions. Pretty soon Doug came back, looking grim after seeing Kim in intensive care. What with all the talking and crying and hugging and kissing, it was a wonder they didn't throw us all out for disturbing the peace.

I didn't have much time to think with all that going on. Even the ride home was a constant nervous chatter, although everyone was pretty done in by then.

But late that night, after everyone finally went to bed, I lay awake for a long time, staring up at the ceiling, because I had a lot of things to think about.

*Just as I have a lot to think about this night. I stared out the window of the Volvo as Sharon and I cruised down the highway toward Pike County, where her Uncle Joe's farm is.*

*We still hadn't said a word to each other. But that was all right with me because I didn't want her to start asking questions yet. I wasn't ready to tell her the whole story because I didn't know how to tell her. It was too fantastic. Too unreal.*

*I remembered that night when I went home from the hospital. I remembered, then, thinking about the accident and those head-lights coming for us in the storm. The other car must have been doing at least seventy when it ran into the Mustang, and it was no surprise when Sheriff Richy told us that the driver had been killed instantly.*

*But Doug had been killed instantly, too. And in that moment of panic the other part of my brain woke up again to show me something new, another trick it could perform. I could move objects. But that didn't bother me so much. It was the other trick that frightened me. I had brought Doug back to life! How could I have that kind of power? He had been crushed! Every time I recall what he looked like, flattened there on the ground with his car on top of him, I get sick. He was smashed like a squirrel on a road! How could my brain put him back together again? How could I rearrange his body like that? But that's just what I did. I pushed out in horror at the sight of him and watched in amazement as the parts of his body started to move ever so slightly. I pushed out harder with my mind, willing Doug's body to return to normal. His head and face actually popped back into place while his chest filled out like one of those inflatable toy animals you blow up. The bones sticking out of him slid back into his skin, and the skin sealed up. All the while, the blood that covered him was washing away in the rain while new blood was being manufactured inside his healing body. I wiped the pouring rain from my eyes and there he was, whole again, as though nothing had ever happened. I stood there staring down at my brother with a mixture of joy and wonder and relief — and terror at what I'd just done. I fell on my knees and gathered Doug's limp body into my arms and started crying. I'd brought him back to life! I'd actually saved him!*

*But I had a feeling that I'd done more than that, because my clothes had been torn up like his. There was even a hole in my shirt, and blood, and I could imagine what that meant. When the other car hit the Mustang, I had been standing next to Doug. And I was beginning to think that I had been killed as well. It was starting to dawn on me that maybe my mind put me back together all on its own because, like Doug, I didn't have any marks on me either. If that was true, it meant that I could never die in an accident. That this fifth power had made me immortal!*

*After I saved Doug, I was going to run over to Sharon and Kim and use my power on them, but it was as if my brain had used up all of its energy, and everything started spinning and growing darker, and then I guess I passed out.*

*I looked back over at Sharon as she sat behind the wheel of her mother's car. I had had to lie to her about her seeing Doug dead. She'd never believe what really happened if I told her, so why bother? Just as she'd never believe what was happening to me tonight.*

*She kept her eyes straight ahead on the road, never saying a word. As far as she was concerned, we were out for a midnight ride. That was fine with me. That's the way I wanted it.*

*I became aware of what was playing on the classical station on the radio. It was a piano and violin duet. It reminded me of how Stephanie and David used to perform together. But they'd never be able to play again, would they? Not now or ever.*

*I turned my attention back out the side window and wondered what I was going to do now that I couldn't go back to town. Now that they were after me. I wondered if it would do me any good to pray. Just as I prayed when I went to church that next day . . .*

the looks of them, there's no way you two could have come out of that accident without a mark on you."

"I guess we were standing far enough away from the Mustang when it got hit —"

"Then you boys wear some pretty messed-up clothes when you're out with your girls."

"It was raining and —"

"I'm not just talking about their being dirty. You and your brother had holes in your clothes. They were ripped. There was blood on them. I saw it."

I shrugged and didn't say anything.

The detective studied me for a second, then said, "I talked to both your girlfriends at the hospital while I was there. Kim Delaney can't remember anything, but Sharon Baker said she saw your brother —"

"I know. She saw Doug under his car. I told her she was seeing things. The shock of the accident and all that."

"Could be. Could be that. But we examined the Mustang and the car definitely rolled over on its right side when it was hit. The wet ground at the accident site also showed the Mustang was knocked on its side. And we found a button from your brother's shirt where the impression is. But what we can't figure out is how the car rolled back on its wheels."

I thought fast. "Wind from the tornado?"

From Sergeant Coffee's expression I could see he hadn't thought of that. He said noncommittally, "Could be." He looked at me as though he knew I was keeping things from him. Then he sighed and said, "I think I'll ask your brother a few questions. Is he up to it?"

"Sure. I'll get him."

"No. That's all right. I'll go inside and talk to him. Don't want your folks thinking what I'm doing is top secret or anything."

We went inside, and Sergeant Coffee asked Doug his interpretation of the accident. After a few minutes of getting nowhere, he left.

"What's he after?" Doug asked.

"I'm not sure," I replied as I headed for the kitchen to get a glass of milk. "The accident doesn't have anything to do with Dave's disappearing, I know that much."

Dad said, "He knows what he's doing. That's his job."

Then Ivy said, "You guys get the feeling he suspects something about the accident?"

"Like what?" Mom asked.

"I don't know. Something, though."

Ivy was right. After Sergeant Coffee had gone, I was sorry I hadn't pushed out and read his mind to see what he was thinking. My powers were so new, I sometimes forgot to use them.

Doug and I drove over to St. Mary's Hospital in Mom's car. We both walked into Sharon's room. Doug gave her a quick hello, then went to visit Kim. That left Sharon and me alone in the room. I leaned over and put my hand on her face. "Hi."

She smiled up at me and her voice sounded soft and tired. "Hi."

"Where is everyone?"

# 13
# The Grief-stricken Woman

The morning after the accident, Mom and Dad told Doug
and me that we didn't have to go to church if we didn't
feel like it, but we wanted to go because we had an awful
lot to thank God for. We were all alive. Sharon had been
lucky enough to only get banged up a little. Kim hadn't
been so lucky. But at least her skull fracture was minor,
and she was awake and talking, according to the hospital
when Doug called.

I had my own reasons for wanting to go. I wanted to
ask God what was happening to me. My powers were
becoming too frightening. I could maybe handle the first
four, but the fifth one — I had to know why I could bring
the dead back to life. So the five of us walked to church,
not saying much, each of us reflecting on what had
happened — and what could have happened. I know Ivy
thought about that a lot. She even alternated holding my
hand, then Doug's, as we walked down the street. She
had gone through quite a trauma, and the thought of
losing both her brothers had almost done her in.

In church, I prayed with all my might for an answer to
my questions. And then I glanced over at Doug and
thanked God again that he was sitting there beside me.
If I hadn't had the power to save him — well, I didn't
even want to think about that.

As we walked back home, the subject of the tornado
came up, and I noticed Mom getting a little pale. Then

the topic of Doug's car came up — how it was totaled and how he had to get a new one — and Mom got even paler over that. I pushed my mind out to her and saw her thinking all sorts of horrible thoughts about Doug's car and what could have happened if we had been inside it. Then I decided to push out again and give her a mental command to relax and enjoy the walk home. Just like that, she did relax and acted more like her old self. I gave the same order to Dad and Ivy and Doug, and it was as if a great weight had been lifted from them. We walked down the street almost as though nothing had happened, chatting about one thing and another. Maybe it was a little underhanded of me to do that to them, but they'd gone through enough, and there wasn't any point in their dragging their troubles with them on the walk home.

When we got to our house, who should be waiting for us in his unmarked Ford but Detective Sergeant Coffee. He got out, trying to make his smile appear unofficial. "Howdy, everybody. Sure is a nice morning for walking."

I hurried up to him. "Is it David? Did you find him?"

"No. Sorry, Steve. But we're still trying."

My parents came up and Mom introduced Dad to the policeman.

Sergeant Coffee smiled at Dad. "Hi, Mr. Taylor. Glad to meet you. Sure is fortunate for you and your wife about your sons coming out of that accident like they did."

"I know," Dad replied, putting one hand on Doug's shoulder and the other on mine. He wore the expression of a combat soldier who had made it through a tough battle. "You don't have to tell me how lucky we all are."

Sergeant Coffee nodded. Then he said, "I came over to talk to Steve about a couple of things. Would you mind if I borrowed him for a minute?"

Dad asked, "Is it about his friend David?"

"Yes, sir. We're double-checking a few things, hoping a piece of information might shake loose. You know, sometimes somebody knows something and it doesn't come out the first time."

"I understand. Sure. Go right ahead. And I want you to know how much we all appreciate what you're doing."

I watched everyone go into the house, then turned to Sergeant Coffee. "You still don't have any leads at all about where Dave could be?"

"No. Wish I did. There's some mighty peculiar things about this case I wish I could make sense out of."

"Like what?"

"Well, I'm convinced now your friend didn't run away. And I'm pretty sure he wasn't kidnapped or harmed by some kook."

"Then what did happen to him?"

He raised his eyebrows and shrugged. "That's the sixty-four-thousand-dollar question." He rubbed a finger under his nose, studying me. "Your friend has a lot of drawings in his room, doesn't he?"

I nodded, studying him back. "David paints all the time."

"There was one," he said, "that was a sketch of something pretty strange."

I didn't say anything.

"Most of David's pictures are traditional," the detective went on. "Landscapes, houses, sunsets — you know, that sort of thing. And now there's this picture that looks like a creature from outer space. Here. Take a look."

He reached into his car and pulled out the drawing I'd already re-created in my room. He handed it to me and I stared down at it, feeling a chill break out all over me. Because this one was in color. The creature was blue with large golden eyes. Funny, how I already knew it would look like that. There were so many things I knew, so many things I could do — and didn't realize until they were happening. I tried to keep a poker face.

Sergeant Coffee squinted at me. "Now why would your friend draw something as weird as that? That wasn't his style, according to his parents."

All I could do was shake my head.

He regarded me a bit more closely. "But there're some more strange things going on around here, aren't there?"

I asked cautiously, "What do you mean?"

"Sheriff Richy knows I'm on this case and he told me about your accident. I'm glad none of you kids were killed. I guess you know the guy who ran into you was drunk."

"I didn't know, but it doesn't surprise me."

"Yeah. He was drunk, all right. Whiskey and wheels don't go together, especially in a storm." Then he eyed me like a professional detective. "Doctors told me about your clothes and your brother's clothes. They said, by

accident, had taken all the laughter out of them. They just sat there on the glider swing, rocking back and forth, not saying a word, their eyes not looking at anything in particular.

Stephanie sat in a lounge chair, her face tense and her eyes closed.

Scott broke the silence first. "So what are we going to do?"

Jill, sitting beside him, asked, "About what?"

"About David, of course."

Our eyes involuntarily flicked over at Stephanie. She didn't move.

Terry spoke up next. "It's funny. You hear about things like this happening to people on the news, but it always happens in other places, to people you don't know. Life has always been so . . . so safe for us." He glanced around at us. "Know what I mean?"

We did and nodded back. Terry went on. "But now life isn't so safe anymore, is it? I mean, if David can disappear, then . . . who knows what could happen to us?"

Roxann shifted uncomfortably beside him. "Oh, come on, Terry," she said, "cut it out, will you?"

"No. I mean it. People do disappear, and they don't always live in New York City or Los Angeles. They can be right here in Summerville. And drunk drivers don't always collide with the other guy; they can aim their cars right at you!"

Jill said, "All right. We've had a pretty good life, all of

us . . . up until now. Did we expect it to go on forever?
Things happen to people. Tragic things. Our turn finally
came up, that's all. David's gone, and we have to stick
together and see this thing through. We can't —"

Stephanie suddenly jumped up and shouted, "Stop it!
Will you stop it! You keep talking as though David isn't
coming back! He *is* coming back! I know he will! He has
to! Oh, dear God, he just has to!"

She ran out of my yard in tears.

"Stephanie!" Roxann and Jill took off after her.

"Let them go," I said as Terry started to follow them.
"They'll talk to her. She'll be all right."

Terry slumped back down in the swing and started
rocking again. He repeated Scott's words: "What are we
going to do?" He looked over at Scott, then at me, helplessly. "What in the hell are we going to do?"

I didn't say anything because I didn't have an answer.

That night, Terry and Jill disappeared.


# 14
# Chaos

The following day, Monday morning, I was in the breakfast room helping Mom set the table when the phone
rang. I recognized Mrs. Hawley's voice immediately.

"Steve! Jill's not home! She wasn't in her room when

I went in to wake her up! Do you know where she is?"

I felt a bolt of electricity go through me. "No, Mrs. Hawley, I don't. What do you mean, she's not home?"

My mom stopped what she was doing and looked hard at me.

Mrs. Hawley's voice went higher. "This morning I went into her room — she's never done this before — I don't know where she is!"

The line went dead.

I stood there holding the phone, frozen.

My mother's hand went to her throat. "Steve? What is it?"

I put the receiver down and turned around slowly. "It's Jill. She's gone. She wasn't in her room this morning."

My mother grabbed at straws. "Maybe she couldn't sleep. Maybe she went out for a walk and —"

The phone went off beside me like a fire alarm. I grabbed it and heard another familiar voice. "Steve? This is Mr. Reed. Did Terry say something to you about going out last night?"

I tried to swallow, but my mouth had gone dry. "What do you mean?"

"Terry's not home!" Mr. Reed tried to control his voice. "He went to bed last night — I saw him go upstairs — but he's not in his room now. He isn't anywhere around. I thought maybe he said something to you about — I don't know — going somewhere or something."

I told him about Mrs. Hawley's call.

"What?" he shouted in my ear. "I don't get it! Why would Terry — Do you think he's with Jill?"

"I don't know, Mr. Reed. Did you call Roxann? Maybe she knows something."

"Yes. I'll call her. I'll call everybody in the group to get to the bottom of this! If Terry disappeared like David —" The next thing I heard was the dial tone.

I'd read in a novel once where this guy said he tasted fear, and at the time I thought the writer was just saying that for effect. But there I stood with a sour taste in my mouth that had to be raw fear.

I looked over at Mom. "Terry's gone, too."

My mom's eyes got wider and wider.

"Mom? I think it's happening again."

I started dialing, but everyone's phone was busy. There was no time for breakfast, and school was out of the question. Mom agreed. She gave me the keys to her Buick and I flew out of the house. I had started to get in the car when the thought struck me. Sharon! I dashed to her house as fast as I could. When Mrs. Baker answered the door, I told her what had happened to Jill and Terry and asked her if Sharon was home. Without saying what we were both thinking, she ran upstairs, then came back down a little slower, a relieved look on her face. Sharon was sound asleep in her bed, which relieved me, too. I thanked her and ran back to my house, jumped in the car, and took off.

I drove over to Scott's house first. He was white as a sheet.

"I don't *know* where Jill is!" he shouted at me as we stood on his front porch. "She wouldn't just walk off like that, and we both know it!"

"All right," I said. "Let's keep calm about this and —"

"*You* keep calm!" he yelled back. "First David disappears! Now Jill! And Terry! Jill wouldn't have gone off with Terry! That doesn't make any sense!" His eyes hung on mine, riddled with fear. "Steve, I don't get it. What's happening?"

I shook my head and said, "I don't know. I'm as stumped over this as you are." Then I said, "Look, I'm going to drive around and see what I can find out. You want to come along?"

"I may as well. I can't just sit around here or I'll go crazy!"

We drove over to Roxann's house, searching the streets along the way. When we went up to her door, I could hear her crying inside. When I rang the bell, she ran up to the door with wide, hopeful eyes. "Steve! Scott! Did you find Terry? Do you know where he is?"

I held out my hands and shook my head. "No, Rox. We don't know where he is."

She threw the screen door open and grabbed my arm, hard. "Steve! We've got to find him! We've got to look for him! Help me, Steve! Please!"

What else could I say? "All right, Rox, all right. Take

it easy. We'll drive around town. Maybe Jill and Terry are together. I don't know. Maybe they're . . . they're . . . Maybe . . ." I was starting to babble, and I had to stop myself.

"Come on," Scott said. "We're wasting time."

We jumped in my car and stopped at Stephanie's house next. She looked as wretched and scared as the rest of us. All she could do was ask the same question we were asking ourselves.

"But why would Terry and Jill go off like that? Do you think they're looking for David? Do you think they know something?" She looked at us hopefully, but our expressions were anything but encouraging.

Scott shook his head. "Terry and Jill wouldn't go off like this if they knew where David was. They'd tell the police first, wouldn't they?"

There was no answer on our puzzled faces. We glanced around at each other. Out of the original seven, there were now four of us left.

We drove from one house to another, trying to find out if any news had come in. Terry's parents were beside themselves with worry, and Jill's parents were frantic. David's parents looked absolutely sick at this turn of events. First their son. Now this. What did it mean?

The police came out in full force, led by Sergeant Coffee. The sheriff's department was called in, too, and a volunteer search party was formed again. By noon, over fifty men were out searching. But that wasn't good enough for the four of us. We went up to the high school and grabbed around seventy kids during lunch hour to start a search party of our own. I'm sure Mr. King, the principal, wasn't too happy, but this was an emergency, and there wasn't any time to ask for permission.

By afternoon, more kids had joined us, and there were over a hundred of us out looking. Scott took a search party and headed for the woods by Red Fox Pond. Roxann's group went downtown and cruised the neighborhoods. Stephanie and her friends combed Lewis Park. My gang looked all over Sutter's Hill and the deserted McCahill Mine, but we didn't turn up anything. Then the twenty-five in my party went over to my house and sat down in my back yard, hot and exhausted. We tried to come up with some kind of rational theory to work from.

The circumstances were the same as in David's case. Neither Jill nor Terry had packed a suitcase or taken any money. There weren't any signs of a struggle or of anyone breaking into their bedrooms. There weren't any notes left behind or anything. They simply disappeared. We went down the list of possibilities. Jill and Terry could have run away together. They could be pulling a prank. Or they could be out looking for David. All of those ideas were just plain ludicrous. Which left us right where we had started: nowhere.

Later that afternoon, as the other search parties drifted back, unsuccessful, we all broke for dinner, then reassembled at my house. Only half the kids came back. By seven o'clock, around fifty people were milling around in the yard, talking, asking questions, coming up with more implausible theories. We were ready to do anything. But we didn't know where to go or what to do next. We were like horses lined up at the gate with no one around to start the race. A feeling of frustration swept over the crowd. Somebody suggested that we double-check the riverbank, even though the police had been over it already. A groan of protest came out of the crowd. We were getting nowhere.

Just then, Sergeant Coffee pulled into the driveway. The crowd stopped talking and watched as the man came up to us. He said to me in a low voice, "Why don't we go for a little walk, Steve? He looked as hot and tired and frustrated as the rest of us.

We strolled out to the sidewalk and headed slowly for the corner.

"I appreciate what you kids are doing," he began. "But there isn't much light left, and I think your friends may as well go on home. We don't need anyone getting lost or hurt stumbling around in the dark."

"But we need to do something while there's still hope of finding Jill and Terry."

He stopped and turned to me, and I didn't have to push out and read his mind to know that he thought there wasn't much chance of that happening. "There's something wrong about this whole thing. I can feel it. First David Voigt, now Jill Hawley and Terrance Reed. There's something going on. It's different from all the run-of-the-mill runaway cases I've handled. Something fishy's going on."

I added, "Especially since Jill goes with Scott and Terry goes with Roxann. I mean, there's no way that Jill and Terry would ever go off together, for any reason. Not in a million years."

"Well, kids have a way of switching boyfriends and girlfriends. You know that as well as I do."

"But not them."

"Of course, we're assuming Jill and Terry are together. It could be that all three of your friends are separated from each other."

"I doubt it," I said with conviction.

Sergeant Coffee nodded. "I doubt it, too. No. There's something else going on around here. Something made your friends leave home. It's not the work of a kidnapper or a loony. It has to be something else. Something from the outside."

"What do you mean?"

"I don't know. Something made those three leave home. Something that their family and friends wouldn't even suspect."

"But I know them! I'd know if there was something going on!"

"Sometimes . . . sometimes there are things — strange things — that happen to people that even their closest friends don't know about."

Sergeant Coffee and I studied each other for a long moment.

"Maybe so," I finally said, and I thought about the strange things that had been happening to me.

He turned around and we headed back. "Tell your friends to hang it up for tonight. And tell them to go back to school tomorrow. The principal understands your concern, but a hundred or so kids leaving school tends to throw teachers into a tizzy. Know what I mean?"

I nodded back. "I'll tell them."

"Good." He leveled his eyes at me as he asked his final question. "Are you positive you don't know why your friends left home?"

I shook my head. "If I knew why, I'd tell you in a second."

"I believe you. But I still get the feeling that you might know something — a little, inconsequential thing — that might throw some light on this mess."

I still couldn't tell him about the drawing of the snake and my dreams. Anyway, how could something in a dream have anything to do with what was going on?

We walked up to his car. "See you later, Steve," the detective said. "Tell your friends that the police will do their job and that they should do theirs — and that's going to school. Agreed?"

"Agreed."

He got in his car and drove away.

I headed back toward my yard and the crowd of frustrated searchers.

Late that night, while the town of Summerville slept, Scott Booth, Stephanie Dyer, and Roxann Powell dreamed about blue snakes with gold eyes who talked to them in a strange language they understood. All three woke up, got dressed, crept silently out of their houses, and vanished into the night.

# 15
# And Then There Was One

Tuesday morning turned into an even bigger nightmare.

"Steve, there must be something you've overlooked. There has to be."

My dad said this as he sat across from me in the living room. Sitting around us were Mr. Hawley, Mr. Powell, Mr. Voigt, Mr. Dyer, Mr. Reed, and Judge Booth. All the mothers were home waiting, hoping, for their phones to ring, to tell them something about their missing children. Sergeant Coffee sat beside my mom.

Any other time, I would have been squirming in my chair, the way everyone was staring at me. But I'd lost every close friend I'd had in the world. All of our group were gone now — except me. I was just as frightened and worried as everyone else.

"Dad, believe me. I've gone over this in my mind a million times and I just don't know what's happening. I've tried to think about it from every angle, but all I do is draw a blank. I'm not a psychic, you know. And I'm not a detective!" I was losing control and I had to make myself settle down.

The eyes of the seven men slid over to Sergeant Coffee. He cleared his throat, rubbed a finger under his nose, and looked at everyone in the room. "I'm almost convinced of one thing," he began. "I don't think your kids have been harmed in any way. For some reason they're running away from home. Or, I should say, walking away from home, because they aren't running away from anything that we know of."

The detective held up his hand as everyone protested. "I know, I know. It's incredible. Impossible. These are probably the happiest, the most well-adjusted kids around. They're all bright, excellent students. They're healthy and normal and they all come from good homes and, from what I've seen, they have kind, loving parents."

Every father fought back the tears welling up in his eyes. I tried to fight back my own.

Sergeant Coffee continued. "The long and the short of it is that your sons and daughters walked out of your homes on their own. Why, I don't know. Nobody seems to. We've looked everywhere for them in town. We've got Missouri and every neighboring state alerted. And tonight we're going to have their pictures broadcast on all the TV stations. If there was any hint of kidnapping we'd have the FBI in on it too, but that's not the case here. No. They simply left your homes, and I'll tell you right now that I've never been so baffled in all my twenty-two years of police work. This isn't a prank your kids are pulling on us. It's something else. And now we're going to have to dig deeper for clues."

Sergeant Coffee turned his attention to me. "Steve, you and Sharon Baker are the only ones left out of your group. But you've known these kids all your life, and Sharon has only known them for a short time, so we're going to have to rely on you to give us the most help. I know you've told me everything you can think of, but it's necessary that we go through it all over again. I want you to tell us about your friends, starting from what all of you did over the summer. I want you to remember any arguments, conflicts, or disagreements they had with each other or anybody else. I want to know anything out of the ordinary that happened to them. I want you to remember any strangers they came in contact with, or anyone outside the group who did or said anything to them that bothered them in any way. I know it's a tall order, but it has to be done. So just lean back and start talking. We've all got to hear what you say in case something rings a bell with any of these fathers. Don't hold back, though. This is one time there can't be any secrets. Understand that? No secrets about anything."

They all stared at me hopefully, and I'd never felt so much on the spot as I did then.

I started talking, describing everything from the first day of summer all the way up to the day before. I began at eleven in the morning. At twelve, Mom served us all a light lunch of sandwiches, and I just kept right on talking while I ate. Every once in a while Sergeant Coffee would ask a question or jot something down, or one of the fathers would ask something, but for the most part, I did ninety-nine percent of the talking, and by two in the afternoon I was finished and had nearly lost my voice.

I'd told them everything I could think of — except about my dreams of snakes that looked like the one in David's drawing. I still couldn't tell anyone about that. I don't know why, but I just couldn't. And, of course, I didn't tell them about my powers.

I was finished, but the men weren't. They thanked me for all the help I'd given them, then they left my house with Sergeant Coffee and went down the street to Sharon's house to have her do what I just did all over again.

I wasn't allowed to go along, but I didn't mind because all I wanted to do was go up to my room and crash. I fell onto my bed, exhausted, thinking about this whole mysterious affair. I knew the answer had to be right under my nose, but I just couldn't put my finger on it. How could the group do something like this — just walk out of their homes without my knowing why? I could understand their not letting Sharon in on whatever crazy thing they were up to, because they didn't know her that well. But *I* should have known. We were best friends, for crying out loud! How could they keep something like this from me? It just wasn't possible!

I had never felt so alone in my life. Sure, I had my parents, and I had Doug and Ivy, but my best friends were gone, and that's a whole different kind of loneliness. But more than that, I was afraid. I didn't know what was happening to them. They were in some kind of trouble, and I had to find out what it was.

I was so tired I couldn't keep my eyes open. I felt myself slowly slipping off the edge of reality into that other world of dreams.

And there were those snake people again and I still couldn't understand a word they were saying.

I went over to Sharon's after dinner. She was pretty worn out from her session with the men, and she was still sore all over from the accident. Her face was bruised and scratched and a little puffy, and her left arm hurt. But she was lucky. Kim would be in the hospital for a long time with her skull fracture.

We sat in the living room with her family, trying to figure out what had happened to our friends, but we didn't come up with anything new. Then Sharon and I decided to sit on the porch and watch it get dark. We rocked back and forth on the swing, listening to the creaking of its chains. The trees were filled with cicadas, their pulsating whine sounding like a thousand tiny high-speed drills. A few lightning bugs darted around in the warm summer air, flashing bright yellow, then burning out like tossed matches. And mosquitoes buzzed around our ears like tiny airplanes. The sky grew paler and darker until a couple of stars blinked on, and a full moon played hide-and-seek behind the branches of a mulberry tree by the street. A few people out for evening strolls passed by, and we waved to those we knew. Once again, it seemed as though nothing had happened in our quiet little town, and life just kept flowing on like an endless river.

But Sharon and I knew something sinister was going on, something that happened when it got dark, something that took our friends away in the middle of the night.

Sharon's voice broke into my thoughts. "Steve? What if . . . what if you disappeared next? Did you ever consider that? You're the last one left, and —"

"Yeah, I've thought about it. So has everyone else. Sergeant Coffee wants me in before dark. My dad put locks on my windows and a latch on my door. He even wants me to sleep with my .22 loaded and next to my bed."

Sharon gripped my arm tightly. "Oh, Steve, I'm so scared. I don't know what I'd do if anything happened to you. You've got to be careful. You're going to be next. I know it! I just know it!"

I patted her arm. "No, I'm not. Don't worry about that. Nothing's going to make me vanish into thin air."

"That's funny," she said in a strange voice. "That's exactly what Roxann said to me yesterday . . . just before she disappeared."

We looked at each other; and even though it was hot out, I felt a chill run over me.

And every cicada in town kept screaming and screaming and screaming . . .

*   *   *

Nothing happened that night. I locked myself in my room and woke up the next morning just as I always did. I slept like a log, but I could tell by Mom and Dad's slightly bloodshot eyes that they hadn't slept as well.

I went to school the rest of that week, but I was only going through the motions. I couldn't concentrate on anything, and I guess my teachers knew that because they avoided calling on me. Eating lunch was worst of all because our regular table in the cafeteria was empty. And no one else sat there — I guess out of respect for their missing fellow students. At first I was constantly mobbed in the halls by kids wanting to know the latest developments, and, of course, everyone was telling me how sorry they were. Mr. King called me into his office and had a chat with me, and the counselor assured me that any time I needed him, his door was open.

People were simply being as nice as they could be. But by Friday most of the kids just smiled at me and mumbled something and went their way. I could see it in their eyes; they knew the others weren't coming back. Ever. And now I was to be pitied and left alone to lick my wounds.

On Saturday I found myself mowing the lawn and scrubbing out the trash cans and washing Mom's car, as though it were any other weekend.

But this wasn't going to be just another weekend. Not even close to it.

# 16
# The House on Chestnut Street

It happened that night.

Sharon called and said she didn't feel well enough for me to come over, and after I hung up, I started feeling pretty miserable and alone. I was so used to calling David and Terry and the others to see what they were doing, and now there wasn't anyone to call.

It was around seven. I didn't feel like tagging along with Doug while he went over to St. Mary's to visit Kim. Mom and Dad saw that I was in the dumps, so they did their best to cheer me up. The four of us walked over to Greenleigh's for ice cream, but all that did was remind me of the day my powers started to develop. I tried to act as if I was enjoying myself, but it wasn't easy. It's pretty hard to smile when your world is falling apart all around you. I was halfway through my hot fudge sundae when I started slowly stirring the ice cream around in my dish, turning it into a swirling mess.

"Not hungry?" Mom asked as casually as she could.

I lifted my eyebrows and let them down with a sigh. "I guess not." I let go of my spoon and pushed the glass dish away.

Dad winked at me with feigned amusement. "What? You turn down ice cream? History's being made." He glanced around at the three of us and saw that his little joke had fallen flat.

I said, "I don't know. Maybe I should have stayed home."

Ivy looked perturbed. "A lot of good that's going to do you. You know how you keep saying that Doug has to roll with the punches? Well, you're going to have to start practicing what you preach. You have to keep going, Steve. Even if they never do find your friends. So you may as well finish your ice cream and act like you're alive."

I looked at Ivy and something special passed between us. I was the one who was always giving her my big brother advice, and here she was giving me hers. I suddenly realized how lucky I was to have a sister like her. And, to make her happy, I finished my dessert.

When we got home, I asked Ivy if she'd like to go for a ride. Her face lit up with surprise. "What? You really mean it?"

"Sure. Go tell Mom we'll be back in a little while."

She gave me a big grin, displaying all her expensive orthodontal work. "Wait here!" She dashed into the house and back out in a second. "All set! Let's go!"

We drove out of town because I wanted to get away from everything. We went past the farms stretched out on the Missouri flatlands, and the more miles we put between us and Summerville, the better I felt. Until we reached the place where the accident happened. I slowed down and saw that the shoulder off to the right was still dug up from the impact. And even though both wrecked cars had been hauled away, I could still see them lying there in my mind: one upside down, the other on its side.

I was doing a bad job of running away from my problems. They seemed to be all around me.

I pulled over and turned off the ignition. Ivy and I got out, looking back at the accident site. I said to her, "I've been thinking about what you said earlier. You're right. My friends are — Who knows? Maybe gone for good. Maybe I'll never see them again. I don't know. But you're right about me. I have to keep going, even if it kills me."

The corners of Ivy's lips curled up, just a little, as she said. "I'm glad, Steve. I hate to see you like this. Then you're going to be all right?"

I nodded back. "Yeah. I think so. At least I'm going to try."

We didn't say anything for a few seconds. Ivy looked out at the farmland stretched around us. She said, "I'll bet that tornado scared the daylights out of you, didn't it?"

Out there was the path it had made, like an immense plow, cutting a wide path through the cornfields, over a farmhouse and barn that had exploded like two wooden bombs. Luckily, no one had been home at the time. The debris was scattered everywhere.

"It wasn't the tornado that scared me so much," I said, envisioning Doug's mangled body lying there on the ground. "It was —"

Ivy waited. "What?"

I bent down and stuck a blade of wild grass between

my teeth. "Ivy. What if I told you that —" I couldn't do it. I wanted to tell her about my powers and how I had saved Doug and about my snake dreams. But I couldn't. Something strong inside me that I didn't understand told me to keep it all to myself.

"Tell me what?" she repeated.

"Nothing. It's nothing. What do you say we head on back. It's getting late." I stood up. "Oh, by the way."

"Yeah?"

"Thanks for coming out here with me. I needed that."

Ivy looked at me with a sisterly smile in her blue eyes. "It was nice. We should do this more often."


When we walked into the house, Mom said, "I don't know who's playing silly games, but the phone's rung twice tonight, and every time I answer it they hang up. Would you get it the next time it rings? I don't want to go through this a third time."

I said, "Why don't you let Dad answer it? He can tell them where to get off just as well as I can."

"Your father's next door helping Mr. Stewart fix his lawn mower."

Ivy added, "And probably helping him kill a few beers."

Mom gave a knowing nod. "Probably so."

Normally Mom would have gone over to the Stewarts' with Dad. She and Mrs. Stewart liked to talk about flowers and recipes and things like that. But one of them was always near me these days, just in case. But I wasn't too worried about my vanishing like the others. Any crazy guy who came after me would have to contend with my new powers, and I wondered what I could do if I really ripped loose with them.

Mom had just sat down in front of the TV when the phone rang. I answered it in the kitchen. What I heard sent an electric jolt through me.

A voice said, "Steve? This is Scott. Meet me at the house that's for sale at 532 Chestnut Street, at midnight. Don't say anything to anyone about this, understand?" He hung up.

I was numb all over, and I felt the blood drain from my head.

Mom looked over at me across the living room. "The same person, eh? Somebody must be awfully bored." She turned back to the television set and forgot the whole thing.

I went up to my room, closed the door, and sat on the edge of my bed in a state of shock. It was Scott! He was alive! But he sounded different. Not quite the same. Something no one else would have noticed except me. I couldn't quite put my finger on it. His voice was a little stiff, a bit cold. It lacked the friendliness and humor it usually had. And I didn't like the warning tone it had when he told me to keep quiet about meeting him.

Why was Scott being so mysterious? What was he up to?

I thought about calling Sergeant Coffee, but again, something told me not to. And I started to wonder what that something was.

\*    \*    \*

I waited until I heard my dad snoring, then I got up and dressed in the dark and slipped out of the house. I walked down Dartmouth for two blocks, crossed over to Elm, then over to Chestnut Street. A half block down I spotted the house Scott had mentioned. I stopped and carefully scanned the neighborhood. Everything was quiet except for a dog barking not far away and the sound of tree frogs everywhere. A street light a few houses down cast shadows in black puddles along the dark street. Nothing moved. The windows of all the houses stared back at me like blind men.

I crept toward the house.

It was an old two-story white frame with a For Sale sign staked in its lawn. I went up to the yard, glancing around nervously. Where was Scott? I wondered. And why was he playing this cat and mouse game with me?

Suddenly the front door opened. A dark figure appeared.

"Scott?" I whispered. "Is that you?" I took a step forward, then another, and another, and the closer I got the more it looked like good old Scott Booth standing there alive and well!

"Scott! It's you!" I ran up and almost hugged him, I was so overjoyed. Then I backed up a few steps. He wasn't smiling at me the way I'd expected, and his arms hung limply at his sides.

"Come on in, Steve," he said in a flat voice. "There's something I want to show you."

# 17
# Metamorphosis

I stepped into the deserted house, and the smell hit me immediately. I first noticed it coming from Scott, but it was stronger once we went inside the dark living room. It wasn't a human smell. It was more like a wild animal odor. But I'd never smelled anything like it before.

Scott started toward the back of the house. "Follow me, Steve."

"Where are we going? Scott? What's this all about?"

"You'll see. Stay close."

I followed him across the empty room, hands out in front of me, groping in the dark. He opened a cellar door and I heard his shoe clump on a wooden stair. There wasn't a light on anywhere.

"Watch your step," he said, then started down with me right behind.

I was scared. Really scared. But I couldn't stop myself. I had to find out what was going on.

Three things struck me as I descended those stairs. It felt as though I were being swallowed down a large dark throat, into an even larger and darker stomach. But that was just my nerves playing tricks on me. What wasn't my imagination was the stronger animal stench coming up the stairs from the basement. By the time I neared the bottom step, my stomach started doing a slow roll from the stink. And I had an eerie feeling that there was

wasn't a coincidence. I think you're beginning to realize that now. I mean, isn't it peculiar that all of us have so much in common? The color of our hair and eyes and skin. All those little similarities in our faces. Our immunity to disease. It all adds up, doesn't it, Steve. All of us wondered about it, but we never talked about it much. I think that's because we knew deep inside . . . that we were one."

I leaned over toward Scott, the sweat starting to pop out on my forehead. "What do you mean, that we're one?"

"Just that. You and me and the rest of us. We're all one. We came from the same place."

"From where?" I nearly shouted, becoming more afraid. "You mean from St. Mary's Hospital? Isn't that what you mean?" My heart started thudding in my chest because I knew that wasn't what he meant at all.

He almost groaned at my ignorance. "Oh, Steve. Can't you figure it out? Haven't you guessed by now with all the powers you've got? Damn it, Steve! We're not from Earth! We were brought here from another planet!"

My mouth opened, but nothing came out. Because I suddenly knew way down inside the changing part of me that what Scott said had to be true. But the other part of me rejected it. "No. *No!* NO! It can't be!" I glanced around at the others, and they all nodded their alien heads at me. My voice fell to a whisper. "Dear . . . God . . . no . . ."

Terry mocked me angrily. "Oh . . . dear . . . God . . .

*yes!* And you can leave Him out of this, if you don't mind! A lot of good He'll do you now! Or any of us," he added bitterly, then turned his blue face away with a scowl.

My eyes moved by slow inches from Terry back to Scott. I looked at him pleadingly, wanting to beg him to take back everything he'd said. Or, even more, all the things he had yet to tell me.

"An experiment," Scott said sadly to me. "An experiment conducted by creatures — people," he quickly corrected himself, glancing at David again. "People from another world." He repeated that last sentence more to himself, shaking his head, as though he still couldn't believe it himself. Then he smiled at me, but it wasn't a smile at all. There was too much anguish behind it. "Isn't it funny, Steve? We came from another world. Well? Where's your sense of humor? Why don't you laugh?" His voice broke. He leaned back and wiped a blue-spotted hand over his face. He continued a little more calmly. "I'll tell you about the experiment. Or what little we know. You see, we were created in a laboratory and brought to Earth as embryos."

"Embryos?" I repeated in disbelief. "How? Who brought us?"

David suddenly yelled, "Will you stop asking so many questions! Just listen —"

"I want to know who!" I insisted. "Who did this to us?"

Terry shouted, "Our people! They brought us here

from their world! Our people created us!" He stopped and turned his back on me again, as though to hide his ugliness from me.

The room became electrically charged with a hundred different emotions — too many for me to understand at that moment.

Scott lifted his eyes from the floor he had been staring at and picked up where he had left off. "Our people brought us here in the form of embryos. They implanted us in our mothers without their knowing it. I don't know how they did it. With their powers they can do anything. All we know is, they did it so that we would grow up as normal human beings here on Earth, with human parents."

My eyes grew larger and larger as I listened to this insanity. "What? Are you telling me that . . . my mom really isn't my mother? That my dad isn't —" But, again, the changing part of me knew that what he was saying was the truth.

"It's the same for all of us, Steve." Scott lowered his eyes. "Our mothers and fathers aren't our real parents. We were put together by scientists and machines and chemicals. That's what the experiment was."

I waited for more. Scott just sat there looking down again. "Well?" I demanded. "Go on! Why were we brought here?"

Scott shrugged, averting his eyes from me. "We don't know."

I studied all six of them in turn. No one said anything.

"What do you mean, you don't know? You're telling me we were brought here from another planet, that our parents really aren't our parents, and that you're all changing into those monsters I've been dreaming about — and you don't know why?"

Terry snapped, "Don't call us monsters! And, no, we don't know why we were brought here!"

I squinted at him — not at Terry, but at the alien thing across from me. "LIAR!"

Terry shouted back furiously, "I SAID WE DON'T KNOW!"

"WHY DON'T YOU KNOW?"

"BECAUSE OUR PEOPLE HAVEN'T TOLD US YET!"

I looked over at Scott, and I could tell by his expression that what Terry said was true. And it began to dawn on me why there was so much hostility in Terry and the others.

Then Scott said, "What we do know about the experiment is that our people designed us to have human bodies. But our brains were put together to be half human and half alien."

David suddenly roared, "Don't call our people aliens! They're our people! Our race! We came from them! We *are* them!" He looked away, his gold eyes burning angrily.

Scott glanced at David as he licked his blue-tinted lips nervously. Then he turned back to me. "Anyway, we were supposed to grow up here on Earth as normal hu-

someone waiting for me down there in all that darkness.

When Scott and I walked into the center of the basement, the ceiling lights suddenly flashed on. I was blinded for a second, but when my eyes adjusted to the light, I saw something that horrified me; yet, way back in the corner of my mind, it was something I'd suspected was there all along.

It was the group: all six of them, standing there, staring at me.

And they had all changed.

There were Roxann, Stephanie, and Scott — the least changed of the six — regarding me with yellowish eyes, their skin covered with pale bluish patches like birth marks. And there stood Jill and Terry, who had been missing longer and were changed more. They were a little taller than me now; their eyes were a deeper shade of yellow, their skin turned a solid medium blue. And David — the first to disappear — watched me through suspicious golden eyes. His skin had transformed to a dark blue. His legs had grown longer, and they stuck out of his pant cuffs by at least ten inches, making him nearly seven feet tall. But David had changed in other ways, too. His body was thinner, his head rounder. Patches of hair had fallen from his head, revealing a blue scalp. His hands — which had once painted works of art — were blue and wider, with two small stumps on each one that I knew would soon grow into extra fingers. His face had become flat, ugly, almost unrecognizable. David had had the longest time to change, and there was no doubt that he was rapidly turning into one of those snake creatures I'd seen in my dreams.

"The patrol ship was right," David said to the others in a voice that was cold and unemotional. "He still hasn't changed. That's too bad for him."

Jill did a slow walk around me, studying me with her yellow eyes. "But . . . he is one of us, isn't he?" she asked curiously, examining me as though I were a slab of meat.

Terry's thin blue lips replied, "He's one of us, all right. Only he doesn't know it."

Roxann, Stephanie, and Scott looked as if they felt sorry for me. But they also seemed a little scared.

"What — what's going on here?" I stammered, facing all six of them. "What happened to you? Your eyes? Your skin?" I turned to David and saw a horror staring back at me. "David! What's happening to you? You're —" I tried to swallow the fear rising in my throat. "You're turning into one of those snake creatures!"

David winced at my words. "Don't ever call me a snake again," he said evenly, with a chilling stare.

I backed away from him, aghast at the alien sound of his voice.

Then Terry said, "Sit down, Steve. Over there against the wall." It was more of an order than a request. "We have a lot of things to tell you and we don't have any time to waste."

I hesitated for a second. I didn't know whether to run for it or stay. But I knew I couldn't leave, because I suddenly realized that what was happening to my friends had to do with all the strange things that had been happening to me. And I had to find out what they were.

I sat on the floor while the others took their places around me. David curled up on the floor with his elongated blue legs tucked under him, giving him an almost reptilian appearance.

Scott sat next to me. His face, just like Stephanie's and Roxann's, seemed almost apologetic. Jill's and Terry's expressions were indifferent, and David's hideous face kept staring at me with a distrustful wariness.

I gasped. "Scott. What is this? What's happening? I . . . I don't get it."

"Go on, Scott." David sneered. "You tell him. I don't think Steve likes looking at the rest of us." He leveled his gold eyes on me. "Do you, Steve?"

I didn't answer. It wasn't David who asked that question but something that was taking him over.

Scott said to me, holding out his hands, "Steve. I know all these things that have been happening to us have been confusing to you. I don't blame you for being scared. I'd be scared too if —"

"Get on with it," David grumbled. "We haven't got all night."

Scott's eyes went from David back to me. "Steve. There's something you have to understand. And that's . . ." His voice went flat, as though he were a doctor telling his patient that he's dying from cancer. "Steve. You're one of us. You have been all along."

"One of you?" I shook my head. "I . . . I don't get it."

"Steve. I know you haven't changed on the outside like we have and your mind is only half changed, but you are one of us. You have to learn to accept that."

I frowned at him. My voice nearly failed me. "What are you talking about, Scott? Make sense, will you?"

"I'll try to, Steve. What I'm about to tell you will seem incredible. But, believe me, it's the truth."

"What? What is it? Tell me, whatever it is."

Scott glanced around nervously, as though he didn't know how to begin. "Steve, you were the first of us to change. Only we didn't know it at the time because you didn't change on the outside. And you kept the things that were happening to your mind a secret. But when our time came to change, we were told about you: that you were only half changed mentally. And that you were developing your powers just like us." He looked directly at me. "Only you didn't know why you had those powers, did you, Steve?"

"No. I didn't know. And I still don't!"

Scott nodded understandingly. "I'll tell you. You see, we're part of an experiment. An experiment that went wrong."

I looked over at the others in confusion, then back at Scott. "What experiment? What are you talking about?"

"Maybe I should back up a little," he said, glancing nervously over at Dave every few seconds, as if he were looking for approval. "Steve, haven't you ever wondered why the seven of us were born at the same time? It

"You think I'm going to join you and those snake monsters? I'm not going anywhere! You hear that? Anywhere!"

I turned to run up the basement stairs, but my body suddenly froze like a statue.

"You forget," David said in a frigid tone. "We have our powers, too. You're outnumbered. So don't try that again."

A force like a giant magnet turned me around and my legs did a slow shuffle back to where I had been standing. Then they gave out as though I were a puppet whose strings had been cut, and I sat down hard on the concrete floor.

Roxann was sitting next to me. She looked like a frightened little girl caught in a situation she had no control over. "Steve. It's no use fighting. You have to go back with us. You don't have any other choice. *We* don't have any choice! We have to take you back with us."

I felt their powers release me. I could move again. I looked over at Roxann. "But you can let me go if you want to." I turned to each one of them. "You can fly off to wherever you came from if you want to. But let me stay here! Please!"

Roxann flew at me in anger. "You still don't understand what's going on, do you? We don't have any other choice! Our people want you back with them! We have to do what they tell us!"

"But I'm not changing like you!" I argued. "I'm still

human! I'm not turning into a snake —"

"Shut up!" David screamed. "We have our orders! You're leaving with us tonight and that's final!"

Roxann looked at David with frightened alien eyes. They all did. David was in charge, there was no doubt of that, because he had changed the most; none of them wanted to cross him.

Roxann said to me, "They're going to change you, Steve. The way we're changing. It'll be better that way. Then you'll look like us." Her eyes went down to her blue hand. She stared at the two stubs growing next to her fingers with wild and frightened eyes. Then she looked back at me and said in an apologetic whisper, "We don't have any choice, Steve. We just don't have any other choice!"

The group fell silent.

I looked at Roxann, then at Stephanie and Scott. And I thought of how terrified and confused a dog must feel when the sickness of rabies starts to take over its mind as it slips over the edge into madness. Terry and Jill were almost there. David was no longer David Voigt. He was half alien now and changing more every minute.

I still couldn't believe any of this was really happening. I needed time to think. But there wasn't any time. They were under orders to take me with them. David, Terry, and Jill were going to see that those orders were carried out. The others had to go along with them.

I had to get away! But how? I thought of using my power to paralyze them, but no sooner had I thought of it than Jill said, "Don't try it, Steve. You'd be wasting your time. We can cut off your power the instant you use it on us. Anyway, why would you want to stay? You belong with us. With our people. You'll be happier with us there. You'll see."

It was no good. They could read my mind. Control my body. What was I going to do? I was trapped!

While I was thinking that there was no way out, I suddenly heard a loud pounding on the front door upstairs and a voice outside yelling, "Steve Taylor! This is Sergeant Coffee! We know you and your friends are in there! You have one minute to unlock this door and come out!"


# 18
# Escape

Everything happened at once. David jumped up with the others and scowled down at me. "You traitor! You told the police you were coming here!"

"I didn't tell them. They must have tailed me. But that's fine with me because I want out of here!"

His gold eyes flashed like bright coins. "You aren't going anywhere, and neither are the police." Then he turned to the others. "Jill. Roxann. Stephanie. You stay here and guard Steve. Scott and Terry, follow me. We'll put the police to sleep and hide them down here in the basement. Come on."

I knew they could do it without any trouble. Why not?
I could have done it myself.

That thought gave me an idea. The three girls looked
plenty scared as they watched the others take off up the
stairs. Their attention at that moment was anywhere but
on me. When the last person headed up the steps, I
pushed out hard. Before they knew what hit them, all
three fell to the floor, out cold.

I leaped to my feet and darted over to the basement
door leading outside. It was locked! I stood there, trying
to figure out my next move, when I remembered my
power. I pushed out and willed the door to fall to pieces,
which it did. I dashed through the open doorway into the
darkness and ran up the steps leading to the back yard.
A flashlight glared in my eyes.

"Hold it, Steve. Right there. I knew something fishy
was going on here."

It was Sergeant Coffee's voice behind the light. But
there wasn't time to stop and tell him what was happening. I'd be explaining it to him for the next year and a
half. All I could do was say, "Sorry I have to do this, Mr.
Coffee." Then I gave a push with my mind and knocked
him out. He fell like a rock onto the grass.

I started running, running as I'd never run before in
my life. I heard Terry yell, "Steve's getting away!" I
leaped over a low fence and took off through another
back yard and smashed right into a metal trash can. It
didn't fall, but the noise sounded like a Chinese New
Year celebration in the dead of night. All at once, what

seemed like a hundred dogs started barking in the neighborhood. I took off again, hearing David shout something to Terry and Scott behind me.

I dashed down the driveway, out into another street. I was on Sycamore. But where could I hide? I couldn't go home. They'd find me there, for sure. I couldn't go to the police. They wouldn't believe me. I had to do something — and fast!

I started running again. I ran down the sidewalk as quickly and quietly as I could. Every few seconds I glanced over my shoulder to see if they were behind me, but I didn't see anyone. For a minute I thought they'd given up. But I'd forgotten; this was their town, too. They knew every inch and short cut of it as well as I did. Suddenly I saw three dark figures across the street pop out of the shadows on my left.

"There he is! Get him!"

I recognized David's changed voice, and it sounded colder and angrier than before. Suddenly I felt something like a huge magnet pulling at me. The three of them were combining their powers to stop me. But the force wasn't strong enough, maybe because they were so far away. I don't know. It slowed me down, as if I were running through water, but I could move, and I forced my legs to carry me across somebody's yard, into the back. Once I was out of their sight, their power couldn't hold me, and I was off again like a shot.

I flew over a fence, right into the jaws of a Great Dane! I fell over him and he came at me with a growl. I had just enough time to push out and nail him cold.

I was up and over the other fence, cursing people for putting up so many fences.

I didn't want to have anything more to do with cutting through back yards again. It was too hazardous and it was slowing me down.

I dashed out onto another street and saw a car coming. I was saved! I stood in the middle of the street, waving my hands. But the car kept going and nearly ran me down. I couldn't blame the driver, though. I must have looked like an escapee from the cracker factory, flapping my arms and yelling at him because creatures from another planet were after me. Sure, kid, sure. Tell me another one.

I was on Lewis Avenue. But one street was just as bad as another when there was nowhere to hide. I ducked behind a bush and waited. I didn't see or hear anything. I thought maybe I'd lost them. Anyway, it gave me a few extra seconds to pull myself together and try to think of my next move.

Sharon! Maybe she could help me! It was worth a try. I was five blocks from her house. Maybe David and the others would keep searching for me here. I had to take that chance. But traveling by foot was risky. All they had to do was push out and see the aura coming from me — a bright red one for fear, no doubt. They could spot me in the dark like a stop light.

Just then, I saw the three of them across the street, moving like shadows within shadows, trotting down the sidewalk, glancing in every direction. I knew they were doing the very thing I'd thought of: pushing out and searching for the light coming from me. I crept behind a parked car, feeling my heart pounding inside my chest. What I had seen frightened me. There they were, three of my best friends, lifelong pals, wanting to capture me and turn me into a monster like them. I could imagine their eyes, glowing in the dark; three pairs of golden animal eyes floating down the sidewalk, hunting for me.

I stayed crouched behind the car and prayed to God with all my might to save me. I raised my head by inches until I saw the three through the windows of the car. They went to the end of the block and stopped, looking around. I wondered if they had only the same powers I did or if they had more. Maybe, because they were actually changing into those snake creatures, they had developed some powers I didn't have. Maybe they had super hearing or X-ray vision or mental radar. Anything was possible! But they didn't spot me. They turned the corner and disappeared into the night.

I ran through the streets of my neighborhood, racing in and out of the shadows of street lights, looking all around and in back of me. I pushed out to see if I could pick up their auras in the distance, but the streets were deserted. So far, so good.

I was two blocks from Sharon's house when it dawned on me that David and the others could have cut over to Dartmouth to beat me to my house. I stopped and hid in some bushes. I had to play this smart or I would walk into their trap. The three of them could have headed for my house, or they could have gone back to the house on

Chestnut, or they could still be looking for me where I'd seen them last. They could have split up or stayed together. I just didn't know. I went on — slowly, cautiously, hunched over, creeping silently — moving from tree to bush to tree Indian style; hesitating, listening, pushing out, praying. It took a long time to cover one block and even longer on the last one. The closer I got to Sharon's house, the more jittery I became. They could be watching my house and hers. I crept closer, every nerve in my body alert for the slightest movement, the smallest sound.

When I saw my house, I was tempted to dash inside and wake up my parents and tell them what was happening. But, again, by the time I told them the whole story, David and the others could have us all in their power. At least, with Sharon, I might have a chance.

I made my way down her side yard, into the back. All at once, what little courage I had left me. I crept into the open garage and hunched down beside Mr. Baker's Thunderbird and started marking time with the loud beating of my heart. I waited there for a long time, debating what to do next. I don't know how long I waited. Every nerve in my body was tight, like overwound guitar strings, on the verge of snapping. I sat there waiting, waiting — when a cat suddenly came up behind me and meowed and made me nearly jump out of my skin!

That was it! I had to do something! I couldn't sit around hiding like this anymore or I'd go crazy!

I crept up to Sharon's back door and tried the knob. It was locked, as I expected, and there wasn't any point in trying the front door. I decided the only thing to do was to push out and make the door open. Just as I was about to do it, I heard a sound in the kitchen. I looked up. There weren't any lights on. I waited. There was another sound, then the soft click of the lock on the back door being thrown.

The door swung open.

Sharon slipped outside and closed the door quietly behind her.

I took one more glance around the dark yard, then whispered, "Sharon, It's me. Steve."

She hesitated for a second, then came the rest of the way down and stood in the shadows of the moon blanketing the yard in soft, pale light. "Steve? What are you doing here?"

As I walked up to her, she stepped back, out of my reach. I knew I'd taken her by surprise and I had to think fast. I couldn't tell her what was happening. Not yet. So I said to her as casually as possible, "Oh, I couldn't sleep, so I thought I'd go for a walk around the block. I was just passing by when I heard a noise back here and, well, it was you. What are you doing up, anyway? I thought you didn't feel well."

She stood there staring at me, the shadow of an apple tree covering her face. I could tell in the gloom that she was studying me, as though she wasn't sure what to do. Then she said, "I couldn't sleep either. Why don't you come with me, Steve? I was going to go for a drive."

"A drive? In the middle of the —" I cut myself short. That was exactly what I needed: a car to get me away from here. "Hey, that sounds like a great idea. I could use a ride."

We walked out to the front of the house, where her mother's new Volvo was parked. I pushed out and scanned the neighborhood, but I didn't see anyone. We got in, Sharon started the engine, and we drove away.

I scrunched down in my seat a little and kept my eyes on the sidewalks and yards around us. I noticed that the headlights weren't on. "Hey. Don't you think you should turn on the lights?"

The headlights flashed on, throwing a tunnel of light down the street. I still couldn't see anyone.

All of a sudden I started shaking. My nerves had put up a good battle, but they felt as though they were going to lose the war. "What do you say we drive out of town?" I suggested as calmly as I could. "Let's head for the country."

"All right. I was going to drive out to my Uncle Joe's place anyway."

"Your uncle's farm? Why were you going out there?"

"I just wanted to, that's all."

It sounded a little strange to me, but who was I to argue? Her Uncle Joe's farm was about fifteen miles out of town. I could hide there for the night and come up with a plan in the morning. The night was dark and I was scared. The next day, I could think better. All I wanted at that moment was to get as far away as possible.

I noticed how slow Sharon was driving, and it was making me more jittery by the second. "Why don't we go a little faster?" I said. "If a cop sees us out this late, he might get a little suspicious. And you know Sergeant Coffee wouldn't like me to be out at this time of night."

"You're right," she said, and the car speeded up a little.

When we turned onto the highway I said, "Okay, now you can hit it." I felt the car accelerate, whisking me away from danger. "Take her up to sixty-five." I said, breathing a little easier. "Let's get away from here before anyone sees us."

We drove out of town that night as fast as we could, trying not to attract attention to ourselves, and I had this sick feeling inside my gut that I'd never see my family or my town again. But that was a lot better than never seeing Earth again. No matter what happened, I wasn't going to leave my planet with those creatures. No way. I'd go down fighting first.

# 19
# The Barn

I was shot to pieces. I had to relax so that I could clear my head and think straight. I leaned back and let my mind sort of float, and I felt the tension in my muscles starting to ease up a little. And as I relaxed, I remembered everything that had happened to my friends and me from the time I first started changing right up to what was happening at this moment, and I still couldn't believe that any of it was possible. How could I ever convince Sharon that our friends were turning into some form of alien life because of an experiment that went haywire? How could I ever tell the group's families that they would never see their kids again, that they had to leave Earth because they were turning into hideous monsters? And how could I tell my parents that they really weren't my parents? That I was put together in a laboratory somewhere on another world. That I'm half human, half alien. And that I have extraordinary powers, enough to make me some kind of superman.

How could I convince people of any of this? Obviously, I couldn't. So what could I do? My only hope was that the aliens would pick up the others and not even try to find me. Then, when they were gone, I could go back home and — But how would I ever know if they had really left? That was just it. I wouldn't. What if those snake creatures were waiting for me to show up at my house? Then they'd grab me. I wouldn't have a chance. And that meant I could never go back. They could wait for months or even years, if they wanted me badly enough.

But why would they want me? I wasn't changing into one of them. The answer was obvious. I knew too much. I could tell the authorities — the army, the government, anyone who would listen to me — about them. But who would believe a crazy story like this?

I felt the car slowing down. "Are we there?" I blinked myself back and focused on the farm appearing outside my window. "Is this your uncle's farm? That's funny, I thought it was farther from here." I glanced over at Sharon's face, visible in the dim glow of the dash lights.

"Don't be silly," she said. "I should know where his farm is."

She slowed down some more, then pulled off the road onto a gravel path where a mailbox stood. Our headlights splashed over the dark farmhouse and barn and the adjoining sheds as we drove in, and I wondered what her Uncle Joe would say if we woke him up.

We parked in back of the barn and got out. I didn't see any cars or trucks on the place. And I wondered where her uncle's hounds were. Everything was dead quiet. I got out and looked all around, then up. The clear night sky was filled with a million stars. I stared at them, wondering which one — which distant planet out there — was the world I came from. I felt small and scared standing underneath that immense universe. Then I remembered that the aliens were going to come out of that star-filled sky any time now to get the others — and me!

I said to Sharon as she walked around to my side of the car, "Let's go in the barn. I've got something important I want to tell you. Really important."

I knew I couldn't hold it all inside me any longer. It was then or never. Maybe Sharon wouldn't believe my story, but I had to give it a try.

I opened the door to the barn. It screeched on its rusty hinges as though I'd hurt it.

It was dark inside.

So very dark.

We stepped inside, and I put my arms around Sharon

and held on to her as though I were a drowning man hugging a life preserver. "Sharon, you don't know what I've been going through," I said. "It's been so unreal. So horrible. I know you're going to have a hard time believing what I'm going to tell you, but I have to tell you or I'll go crazy."

Sharon just stood there while all these words were pouring out of me, and I wondered why she wasn't putting her arms around me and hugging me back.

That's when I noticed the animal odor overwhelming all the other smells in the barn.

Then the barn door slammed shut and the lights flashed on.

Terry was standing in front of me. "Really, Steve. Did you think we were going to let you get away? You must think we're idiots." His gold eyes glared at me in a cold fury.

I looked around, stunned, unable to move.

There was Sergeant Coffee's unmarked car parked inside the barn. Standing in front of it were Roxann, Stephanie, and Scott, the blue patches on their skin spreading wider on their faces and arms; Terry and Jill, who had become taller, their bodies more changed, their skin turned a darker blue; and David, whose body was molding even faster into the snake I'd seen in my dreams.

I stared at them, then felt Sharon back away from me. I didn't want to look at her in the light because I was terrified of what I'd see. But I couldn't help myself. I had to look. My frightened eyes moved slowly from the others over to her.

My insides turned to water, as though everything in me drained out on the floor, leaving me empty and hopeless.

A large light blue patch covered the left side of her face. And her beautiful dark brown eyes were already half yellow.

All that time in the car, in the dark, I hadn't seen the changes taking place in her. She was one of them, and she had led me right into their trap.

"Sit down, Steve," Terry ordered, "or we'll make you sit down. You may as well start being cooperative, don't you agree?"

All I could do was stand there, numb, dumbfounded, staring at Sharon. She looked back at me with her new, yellowing eyes, and I saw how cold and alien they were becoming. I kept telling myself, This can't be happening. It can't be happening!

"But it is happening, Steve," Sharon said, reading my thoughts.

It dawned on me why she'd spoken so little on our ride over here; even her voice had started losing its natural warmth and had begun sounding as alien as the others'.

Jill said, "For the last time, Steve, sit down!"

I tore my eyes away from Sharon and gazed around at these things who had been my friends such a short time ago. They all stared back at me with their golden animal eyes, and I was stunned at how much they had changed in the past couple of hours.

A force, like an invisible hand, pulled me down to the barn floor. "There," David growled. "That's better."

I looked up at Sharon, shaking my head in disbelief. "No! Sharon! Not you! Not you, too!"

She looked down at me, and I could see the hint of another bluish patch begin spreading on the other side of her face. "I was always part of the experiment, Steve. Right from the beginning, sixteen years ago. Only, like you and the others, I didn't know it until I started changing."

At that moment my heart broke into pieces. Sharon was gone. She was standing beside me, and she was alive; but I felt that she may as well have been killed in the car accident. She was rapidly changing second by second into something that wouldn't be her. Wouldn't be human. And I didn't want to be around to see it happen.

My voice fell to a defeated whisper. "When did you . . . find out —"

"That I was one of you? Tonight. After I went to sleep. That's when I began changing and had the dream. Our people told me about the experiment and how it was going wrong. They told me that all of you were changing like me, that I had to get away before anyone saw me, and that all of us had to meet here to be picked up. I was on my way over here when I met you. You see, our people told me about you, Steve. That you had only partially changed, in your mind, and that you weren't being cooperative about going back with us."

I swallowed, feeling sick inside. "So I fell right into your hands."

She shrugged without emotion. "It's just as well. Our

people would have found you anyway when they came to get us."

"You see, Steve," Roxann said almost sympathetically, "you were going back with us one way or the other, no matter what you did. We tried to tell you, but you wouldn't listen."

I looked at the group, and they looked back at me with their changing eyes, and I knew for certain that this time I was finished.

Terry said, "Everyone in the experiment is leaving Earth tonight before we're found out. Nothing is going to change our plans, Steve. Not you or anyone else. And you're not leaving our sight this time, so don't try anything funny. You're outnumbered seven to one."

"But why do I have to go?" I pleaded. "I'm not changing like you!"

"We already explained that to you." Scott sighed. "Your mind has already changed. You're one of us. Why can't you understand that?"

I looked across the barn at David. He lay on the floor, curled up. And the smell coming from him was awful. His blue legs had become unbelievably long, sticking out of his jeans by about two feet. He wasn't wearing shoes or socks, and his feet were small and round, quickly disappearing. His face was rounder, half human, half alien. I noticed that he was making a strange sound with each breath, a kind of rasping noise through his flattened nose. He just stared at me with his cold eyes like a snake watching its prey, waiting to see what I would do next. He had changed more than the others, which meant he probably had more mental power than they did. He was the one I had to look out for if I was going to try another escape. And I knew he was lying there coolly reading every single thought that came into my head.

Sharon was the least changed. If the others hadn't been there, I could have tried reasoning with her to let me go. There might have been just enough humanness in her to appeal to, but the others were too far gone. It was hopeless. If I had had the power to lift a car, I thought of what their combined powers could do to me if I tried anything.

I was frightened. But I was angry, too. "What are we waiting for, then?" I shouted. "Why aren't your snaky friends here to take us away?"

Roxann answered, "They're our people, Steve. You mustn't make fun of them. Their physical form may seem odd to you now, but you won't feel that way later. You'll be thankful that you're one of us when the change is complete. You'll see that this is much better."

Jill gave me a forgiving look, like the expression a mother gives her child when the child is wrong and doesn't know any better. She said to the others, "It's because his mind's only half changed. He doesn't think like us. But he will soon enough."

I shouted, "But I don't want to change into a monster like you! I'm human! I want to stay that way! I want to stay here on Earth! I'm happy here! And so were you once!" I tried in vain to reach out to them. "Sharon. Terry. Jill. All of you. Don't you see what's happening to you? You were all happy living on this planet. Can't you remember that? Have they screwed up your minds so much that you can't remember how much you love your families? If you can remember, then you know how much I want to stay here. How can you —"

An invisible force clamped my mouth shut. I glared over at David, but he only gave me a curt glance and looked away.

Sharon turned to him and said, "Stop it, David. Let him talk. He *is* one of us, you know."

"No he isn't," David said in a slow, gasping voice. "That's why he's dangerous to us and our people." And then he said something in a foreign language that sounded strangely familiar. It was the same language the snakes had used when they spoke to me in my dreams. I couldn't understand what he said, but the others did, because something had awakened inside their heads that hadn't in mine. Call it an alien soul or spirit or whatever you want. It was the part that made them different and left me still very human.

"Please," Sharon said to David, "release him." She sat down next to me. "He won't say anything to make you angry. He'll promise."

David gave me a chilling stare, and I nodded reluctantly.

The pressure left my mouth. I forced a smile and said, "Thanks." I decided I'd better cool down. Losing my temper wasn't going to get me anywhere. I asked. "When will they pick us up?" That seemed innocent enough.

Stephanie answered, "All we know is what they told us in our dreams. They said they'd meet us at this farm tonight. The people who live here are gone, so it's safe here for now."

Scott added, "When the main ship arrives, it'll wait outside our atmosphere and send patrol ships down to get us. Then we'll be taken to the main ship with all the others."

Terry glanced at his watch. "It's quarter after two. They'd better hurry. There's only a few more hours before daylight."

"They'll be here soon," Jill said. "I can almost feel them coming."

"So can I," Sharon echoed.

"Me, too," Scott said.

The group glanced around at one another, nodding, sharing some understanding that was beyond me; and they all smiled at one another with a far-off look in their alien eyes.

We waited for more than three hours, but it seemed like an eternity.

We sat in the barn, not saying much of anything. The only sound came from the corner where David lay. His breathing became louder, more labored. I tried pushing my mind out to him to see what he was thinking, but the moment I did, he somehow cut me off, and all I got was a kind of mental static. I began wondering if I could cut him and the others off the same way he did me when Terry warned me, "Don't try it." That was all he said. Well, so much for that. Since I couldn't block them off, that meant they could listen in on my brain as though they were watching a television set, and I could do nothing to prevent it.

But I couldn't very well stop thinking. You have to be dead to do that. So I tried talking instead.

"I wonder what kind of world we're going to. I wonder if it's as good as Earth."

"We don't know," Terry replied. His face was uglier and rounder than before, and I noticed his legs sticking beyond the cuffs of his pants. "It doesn't make any difference, though. It's our world, for better or worse."

I didn't want to anger them by responding to that bit of philosophical bull, so I turned to Sharon and asked, "Are you excited about leaving?"

She had been staring at nothing, lost in her private alien thoughts. She sort of shrugged. Her blue-spotted face didn't show anything I could read. "Not in the way you mean. 'Excited' is a human emotion. I don't feel much of that now." She paused for a moment, studying her new feelings. "I'm looking forward to going, though. I want to be with my people, where I belong."

I was getting tired of hearing that response. It was almost as if they were programmed to say it. With every moment that her body changed, I knew her mind was changing, too. But I thought her tone lacked conviction. I attempted to reach out to the human part of her. I leaned over and whispered, "Sharon. Even with all this going on, I want you to know I still love you."

She stared straight ahead with a hint of a smile, and for

a moment I thought I'd touched the old Sharon, still lurking inside that altering body. "Love?" She said it slowly, looking inward, as though trying to recall a place she had been to once and couldn't quite remember. "Love?" She turned her yellowing eyes on me. "I'm fond of you, Steve. I like you. But that's all. Don't expect any more from me than that."

It was like a slap in the face. She was becoming as emotionless as the snake she was turning into.

I said to her with all my heart, "But I still love you, Sharon. Don't you remember how it was between us? We loved each other!"

"You can love me if you want, Steve. If it makes you happy." She went back to staring off into space as though our relationship didn't hold any more interest for her.

Happy? I was heartbroken. Destroyed. All the plans we'd made: finishing high school and going to college together, getting married, having our own house and children — all of it was slipping right through my fingers like so much sand. God, how that hurt. Like nothing I'd ever felt before. The only girl I'd ever loved had turned against me — my whole world was coming apart.

I fought away my tears because I didn't want to show any more emotion around these creatures than I had to. If I acted as cold as they did, maybe they'd trust me a little more. And I needed that if I was going to have any chance of saving myself.

I wiped my eyes, pretending I had something in them. "You're right, Sharon," I said in a low, flat voice. "Love is too human an emotion. Maybe it's better your way."

She didn't say anything. She kept staring straight ahead as her listless eyes grew more yellow and alien by the minute.

It's one thing to lose the people you love when they move away — or worse, when they die; but there I was, losing my friends as I stood by helplessly, watching them change. I looked at Sharon and silently said goodbye to her in my mind. I knew she heard me, but she didn't show it. Then I looked over at Jill and Scott and said goodbye to them; then Terry and Roxann, and finally Stephanie and David. I said goodbye to them just as though we were all at an airport seeing each other off for the last time. I was wishing them farewell, knowing I'd never see them again: at least, not their old selves. They were leaving me, not in distance, but in body and mind. What really hurt was that they weren't saying goodbye to me. No handshakes. No kisses. Nothing.

I didn't know there was that much pain in the whole world.

I watched them change.

As the long minutes turned into even longer hours, I sat on the barn floor witnessing a horror show. Except that this wasn't some Hollywood movie about gargoyles, with all the nifty special effects. This was the real thing happening right before my eyes!

To describe David was to describe what was happening, or would happen, to the others. His feet were gone and his legs had transformed into two long appendages, each one resembling the tail of a snake. His arms had become a bit shorter, his shoulders thicker, his hands wider, and the two extra fingers on each hand were now fully developed. His head was horrible to look at, not so much because it looked like the snake creatures, but because inside that awful Halloween mask was something that still resembled the friend I had grown up with. His lips were gone and so was his nose; there was only a slit and two small holes to replace them. His eyes had grown larger and rounder, and they bulged out like two golden bubbles. His skin remained humanlike, except that it was dark blue. My guess is that he was over nine feet long and growing more by the minute as he lay curled up on the floor.

His breathing grew worse as time went by. After a couple of hours he was almost choking for air. By then, Jill and Terry were starting to gasp a little themselves. With the three of them fighting for air, I realized that their alien bodies couldn't breathe in our atmosphere.

By the time three hours had passed, the situation was becoming critical. David was dying! And that meant Sharon and the others would die too if something wasn't done soon!

I still didn't move or say a word. I watched as the group crawled over to David. They looked down at him, stretched out on the floor, suffering, knowing each gasp for air could be his last. And I knew they realized that their own time was running out, too.

So this was why they and the others in the experiment had to be picked up tonight. Not only because of how they looked, but because our air was poisonous to them.

It made me think about the real reasons for this experiment. What would have happened if their bodies hadn't changed? What was the plan behind all this? Only one explanation was possible. It had to be a plot for some kind of an invasion. That had to be it. The aliens wanted to create a race of beings with human bodies and their brains: a perfect combination to take over our planet. This way they wouldn't have to fight the people of Earth. All they had to do was reduplicate themselves in human form.

They were smart all right, these snakes. But their experiment hadn't worked out. That meant there was time to warn people about their plan. But who would believe me? I'd make them believe me. I could command them to believe me! Then the people of Earth would know what was really going on.

I turned my attention back to David, watching him strangling in a death struggle I couldn't stop. But, then, did I want to stop it even if I could? He wasn't the same person I had once known. He had become a stranger. An enemy. An invader. It was only an alien animal suffocating over there in the corner of the barn. A dying snake. But what made me sick at heart was knowing that the real David Voigt was trapped inside that horrible dying body, and he couldn't get out.

Or could he?

The idea sprang into my head all at once. Of course! Why hadn't I thought of it before? How stupid of me! If I had the power to save my brother — if I could restore Doug's crushed body back to normal — then why couldn't I do the same thing for David and the others?

I was so excited by the idea that I forgot that they probably had heard me thinking it. I watched them and held my breath. They didn't move. They were still around David, their golden eyes turned down at him. Not one of them looked over at me or said anything. I hoped their attention was on their own problems and not on me anymore. So far, so good. If they would only stay that way for a few seconds longer.

I had to hit them with everything I had before they had a chance to cut me off. I concentrated on what I had to do. I began preparing myself, feeling my power rising in me like a giant turbine, building up millions upon millions of volts of energy. It kept building and building and rising until I knew I was ready. Then I pushed out with all my strength, and for a few seconds I was blinded by the force of my own power. I pushed out again and again and again, willing my friends' alien shapes to change back into their original form.

I heard their screams, but I couldn't see them. They cried out like tortured animals, as though the alien part of them was resisting my power. I felt myself growing weak, but I kept pushing and wouldn't let go. I gave one final burst of power and prayed to God that it was enough to do the job, because I felt the energy inside my head giving out. Then I fell back against the barn wall, exhausted and drained.

I felt dizzy and had to wait a few seconds for my head to clear. Finally, I opened my eyes, afraid at what I would see.

All seven of them were lying on the floor, not moving.

And then they started changing before my eyes, just as Doug had done. It was like running the transformation they had been going through backward on fast reverse. I watched as the blue patches on Sharon's skin melted away until her tanned color returned. My heart leaped for joy, and I staggered across the floor and took her in my arms. She gave out a small moan and batted her eyes open. They were dark brown and human again, and when she looked at me, I knew that the real Sharon was back.

"Steve?" She blinked up at me in confusion. "Steve? What . . . what happened?"

I hugged her and kissed her cheek, and I wanted to laugh and cry at the same time. "It's all right. It's all over. You're okay now. You're back. That's all that counts. Oh, Sharon, thank God, you're back."

Scott, Stephanie, and Roxann were the next to revive. The three sat up groggily, their old selves once again, blinking around as if they'd just awakened from a long sleep. Roxann looked over at me with a perplexed expression. Then she examined her hands and arms and looked over at the others. Her eyes opened wide at the realization of what had happened. "Steve? Did you . . . Steve! You changed us back! We're changed back!"

While the four of them were coming to their senses, Terry and Jill began stirring on the barn floor. They had taken longer to return to normal because they'd changed so much. I went over to help them sit up. They were pretty groggy, too, but after a few seconds they started to come around. Terry shook the cobwebs out of his head.

Then he looked up at me, and I saw the last bit of yellow disappearing from his eyes. "You . . . you saved us, Steve," he managed to get out, taking hold of my arm. "I . . . owe you one." He tried to smile.

"Forget it." I gave him a friendly slap on the shoulder. "This one's on me."

I crawled over to where David lay. I couldn't understand it. He wasn't changing at all! I checked out his aura and what I saw confused me. A brilliant gold color radiated from him, pulsating brighter and brighter. It was as though the alien part of him wouldn't let go!

Stephanie staggered over and looked from David back to me. "Steve? You did change us, didn't you?"

I kept my eyes on David and nodded.

"Then . . . what's wrong with him? Why isn't David changing back?" Stephanie gripped my arm. "You've got to do something, Steve! Try whatever you did again! Please!"

"All right," I said. "But I don't know if it'll do any good."

I stood over David for a few seconds while the others watched me in silent concentration. I thought about what these aliens had done to Sharon and me, and I became angry. I thought about what they had done to my friends, and I grew angrier. I thought about this experiment and the nightmare it had put us all through, and I felt a rage boiling inside me. Then I looked down at David and saw what the aliens looked like and what they wanted to turn us into, and I felt myself shaking with fury. And at that moment I pushed out at David with all my might. I

But it wasn't.

For at that moment we felt the earth tremble as something huge and heavy landed outside the barn.

All eight of us realized that it was the aliens.

And they were coming for us.

# 20
# The Aliens

We edged our way to the back of the barn next to Sergeant Coffee's car, huddling together in terror, hearing the muted sounds outside coming closer and closer.

Then the barn door creaked open and an overwhelming alien smell filled the air.

And there it stood: a giant, hideous blue snake with large golden eyes. It was incredibly long, and the upper half of its body was arched, cobra fashion, towering over us, standing ten feet tall. Its huge chest and muscular arms had dark blue plates growing on them, like the armor of some prehistoric animal. It wore a transparent helmet, and behind the glass was a face right out of a nightmare.

It glided into the barn on its thick tail, sounding like something heavy dragging across the wooden floor. Then it halted and glared down at us with its cold, glowing eyes. "Who are you?" it demanded angrily.

All eight of us pressed closer together, hearing the alien's deep voice coming from inside our heads.

"Where are the children in the experiment?" Then it roared, *"I said where are they!"*

But we were so afraid that none of us could say a word.

The giant's eyes became immense, growing into frightening yellow lamps. "I came here to get the children from the experiment and all I see are you humans! For the last time! Where are they? What have you done with them?"

The monster headed for us with a menacing look on its ugly face. We pressed back even more against the hard steel of the car, knowing we were hopelessly trapped.

The thing stopped a short distance from where we stood, looking us over slowly, one by one, then fixed its burning eyes on Roxann and spoke in a voice that sounded like low, rumbling thunder. "All right, human. You tell me where you're hiding them or I'll make you wish you were never born."

Roxann cringed against Terry, her voice hysterical with fear. "Please. Leave us alone. Don't touch me. Don't touch me."

Her body suddenly went rigid as she let out a scream of pain. Her arms slammed stiffly down against her sides as though she were being squeezed in the grip of a gigantic hand. And the beast had done it all without lifting a finger.

Terry broke away from us and shouted up at the giant,

"Let go of her!" and grabbed a pitchfork leaning against the wall next to him. He rushed at the monster to stab it, then suddenly let out an agonized yell of his own and flew up into the air and hovered there with his arms locked at his sides. The next thing we knew, the pitchfork disintegrated in his hand and fell to the floor in tiny pieces. Then we watched in stunned horror as Roxann rose into the air beside him.

The creature grinned with evil delight as its mind held them prisoner.

Then both of them began moving toward each other, high in the air, then away, then toward each other again, like helpless puppets swinging back and forth on invisible strings. We realized that they were swinging closer and closer toward each other, and we suddenly knew what the monster was going to do to them!

"Now you'll tell me what you've done with them, won't you? *Won't you?*"

Just as the monster was about to smash Terry and Roxann into each other, another deep voice from somewhere roared, "Stop that, you fool! I command you to put those humans down at once!"

Our heads jerked toward the open door only to see two more aliens entering the barn.

The giant regarded the newcomers with a disgusted look darkening its face.

"I said put them down now!" one of the aliens repeated.

For a short moment, nothing happened; then, as if by

magic, Roxann and Terry floated back down and collapsed onto the floor in a heap.

We all rushed over to see how they were. Luckily, they were only out of breath and badly shaken.

In the meantime, the two new aliens moved up to where we were and I could see the difference among the three immediately. These new creatures were shorter and slimmer than the first one, and their skins were smooth and a lighter shade of blue. When I looked them over, it seemed that the smaller of the two could have been a female, while the bigger one must have been a male.

"You military people make me sick," the male snapped at the giant.

The giant glared back at the male with restrained anger. "I was only doing my job," he growled defensively.

"Your job doesn't include killing innocent humans! Those days are over with, soldier!"

"Human beings." The giant scowled with contempt. "Look at them! Nothing but ugly monsters!"

"I'm sure they would probably say the same thing about us," the female replied with a touch of irony in her voice.

The male waved his blue hand at the giant. "Leave us."

"Leave? My orders are to —"

"Your orders are to obey my orders! Or have you forgotten who is in charge now? Go on. If we need you — which I doubt — we'll call you."

The armor plating on the giant's skin actually swelled outward as its immense muscles tightened with quiet rage. Then it gave the eight of us one last vicious glare with its bright yellow eyes, and glided out of the barn with amazing speed.

We regarded the pair of aliens left behind and saw them looking back at us with relatively kind faces.

"Please," the female said, "don't be afraid of us. My husband and I want to apologize for the behavior of the guard. He's a soldier and — well — their methods are somewhat crude at times."

"Crude!" Terry barked as he helped Roxann to her feet. "That guy wanted to kill us!"

"You needn't worry about that now," the male assured him. Then he took us all in with his golden eyes. "We have a serious problem on our hands. We must find the children who were in the experiment before it's too late. And since you're here, I must assume that you know what children I'm talking about."

None of us moved or said a word.

"I know how afraid you must be," the female said, "but we're asking you to trust us. We've got to rescue the children now. We created them, and we're responsible for what happens to them. Please, help us save them before they die."

Again, we didn't say anything.

"Why are you hiding them?" the male asked. Then he moved a little closer to us. "Or *are* you hiding them? He peered down at us, his eyes slowly examining each of us in turn, and I saw the surprise growing in his face. I felt a funny sensation inside my head and I suddenly realized he was probing our brains!

"*You* are the ones!" he exclaimed. "Aren't you?"

I glanced around at the others, and it was written all over our faces that they had us cold. How could we have ever hoped to hide anything from these creatures when they could read our minds like books?

I tried to appear brave even though I was shaking inside, and I took a step forward, feeling Sharon trying to pull me back. "All right," I said. "So now you know. So what happens to us now?"

The female's brow wrinkled down at me. "But how can this be! None of you has begun the transformation!"

"We started to change," I told her, "only I reversed the process and changed my friends back to the way they were."

The male recoiled in amazement. "*You did what?*"

"I said I changed them back to normal human beings."

"You? But how did you do it?"

"What do you mean, how did I do it? You should know. I was given the power, so I used it." I found myself growing angry. "Come on! Did you really think I was going to just stand around and watch my friends turn into snakes without doing something about it? You must think we're —"

"Power?" The male interrupted me. He leaned his reptilian body down even closer, staring at me. "What power? We never gave anyone in the experiment an ability such as that. Even we cannot reverse the process once it has begun."

The pair glanced at each other, mystified.

"Could it be?" the female asked her husband. "Is such a thing possible?"

He shook his blue head. "I don't know. It could be. Anything in this ridiculous experiment is possible. Didn't I warn them not to try it? Didn't I tell them that mixing our genes with human genes would create genetic mutations we couldn't even dream of?" He turned back to me. "If you have developed such a power, then it's a good thing the guard didn't find out about it. If he had reported this to his general —" He hesitated, and another worried expression crossed his face.

My mind was going a mile a minute, trying to make sense out of it all. "Okay," I said. "Now you know about me and my friends. So what happens now? Do you change us back into monsters? Take us away from our world? Or just kill us? Come on! Tell us your next move, so we at least know what we're in for!"

Both aliens blinked their windowshade eyelids down at me, surprised at my outburst.

Suddenly, I wasn't afraid of them anymore. I knew they weren't out to hurt us, but that didn't mean they didn't have other plans for us. Then I thought of pushing out with all my might and trying to knock them out so we could have a fighting chance to escape.

"No," the female said, reading my thoughts, "you

needn't do that. We have no intention of harming any of you."

I tried to calm down, knowing that I had to understand what was happening. "Then tell us. Why did you do this to us? Why the experiment? What are you doing here on Earth? What's this all about?"

The creatures glanced at each other, and it was the female who answered. "The experiment," she said slowly. "The atrocity, you mean. We were going to tell you about it when we got you back to the city-ship with the others. But I suppose you may as well know now. Open your minds, all of you, and I will tell you every-thing."

It was as though I had gone to sleep standing up, and the next thing I knew I was dreaming. No. It was more than a dream. I was actually projected into another di-mension: a place of thoughts and images and feelings. A world somewhere between dreams and reality.

I found myself floating in outer space, trillions of miles from Earth. I was alone, suspended in eternal darkness, with no air or gravity, surrounded by an endless pan-orama of stars that I knew was the entire Milky Way galaxy. I'd never seen anything so vast and beautiful. Stars and planets were all around me: a billion billion pinholes of silvery light shining across the never-ending silence of measureless space.

Suddenly, to my right, one of the lights moved among all those motionless stars. It grew in size, and somehow I knew it was a planet that had been wandering through space for billions of years. I watched it coming closer, becoming larger, and I realized that it was heading right for me! I threw my hands out in front of me in a meaningless gesture to protect myself. I screamed, but no sound came out of my mouth. All I could do was hang helplessly in space and watch the planet rushing toward me, faster and faster!

It was red — a hellish, burning red — and it rotated through space like a gigantic ball of fire rolling along an invisible floor. It missed me, passing directly in front of me, so close that I thought I could almost reach out and touch it. It was so unbelievably huge that, floating beside it, I felt reduced to the size of a mere dot. It was so immense that it blocked out the space where half the universe had been. I could see thousands of volcanoes on it as it went by, all of them erupting, blasting out a crisscross of liquid fire that flowed in angry smoking rivers over the planet's craggy surface. And, as the planet passed me, I spotted a green planet in the far distance on my left.

I suddenly found myself on the surface of this other world. I stood in a valley of gently rolling hills, dotted with flowers made of delicate, colored glass. Lime-green mountains rose all around me, and great waterfalls of liquid silver spilled out of them, cascading down and down thousands of feet, splashing into cool streams where lemon-yellow fish leaped and played. Large birds coasted in the air on thin crystal wings, making lazy circles in a lavender sky. Shiny blue trees shimmered in a breeze, their triangular leaves spinning on branches like toy windmills. Two small suns hovered over a platinum sea, shimmering on the rippled surface like scattered diamonds.

The dream scene changed.

I was on top of one of the green hills and it was growing dark. But I wasn't alone. I was surrounded by the aliens. Thousands of them — tall, blue, horrid —standing upright on their flat tails, their hideous faces lifted toward the sky, their expressions stamped with dread. I followed their glowing gold eyes up where they pointed, and they whispered in terror-filled voices. Out there, among all the early evening stars, I saw what they were looking at: a round object bigger than all the other lights in the sky. It was red, and it was growing larger.

A moan, a weeping, a cry of utter despair, poured from their throats, and I knew why they were watching the sky. The red planet I'd seen in space was on a collision course with their planet!

It was the next day in the early morning. I was on the crest of a green hill, overlooking a strange and distant city teeming with soaring towers and spires. The entire complex was made of a polished metal that caught the light of the twin suns, flashing it back in my eyes like thousands of giant mirrors. I looked up and saw the glowing red planet, looming larger and more ominous now, burning a hole in the soft lavender sky.

Suddenly, the ground shook. Hundreds of flying creatures took to the air like thrown jewels. To my amazement, I saw the metal city slowly lift off the ground, its massive weight rising into the air. On the ground were crowds of blue aliens, their long necks craning upward, watching with sad and frightened eyes as the only survivors of their civilization escaped the imminent destruction they had been left behind to face. High in the cloudless sky the city-ship fled, faster and faster, in the opposite direction of the red circle that was growing larger and larger as it rushed down on them.

I was in space again — a tiny human speck in the vast expanse of the universe. Before me, on the right, was the giant red planet, tumbling through space, out of control. To my left was the aliens' planet, floating serenely in its orbit, just as it had done for countless centuries.

Both worlds prepared for a battle to the death.

The closer they came, the more both spheres bulged out toward each other. At first their magnetic attraction caused the platinum seas to rise up from the green planet in one long silvery stream that stretched for thousands of miles, bridging the great gulf between the two worlds. The seas washed tidal waves over the oncoming red planet, trying to put out its volcanic fires. Then their gravitational force caused the red planet's side to burst open like a great bloody wound, heaving an ocean of molten lava from one planet to the other, like an immense flame thrower, setting the green planet on fire. Then, in slow motion, their surfaces touched, as erupting volcanoes collided with green mountains. Like two giant ships, they drove into each other, their titanic weight carrying them ever forward with destructive momentum. They began melting into each other in a series of tremendous explosions: first their two surfaces fusing together, driving deeper and deeper into each other, until a mammoth ball, half red, half green, blended together for one brief moment. But they didn't stop there. They couldn't. Their momentum forced the planets to keep ramming into each other until, at last, they blew up in one final colossal explosion, sending billions of fragments great and small flying off in all directions to scatter among the stars.

Where the two planets had been, only a smeary rainbow of cosmic dust remained. Where a civilization of aliens had once lived, only a cloud of vaporized matter floated in an insignificant nebula.

Again the dream changed.

I was following the city-ship as it flew through space, and I heard the female alien speaking in my head.

"Our world was gone, and so the survivors of our race searched the galaxy for a new one. We searched for years and more years . . ."

I followed the city-ship as it flew by planets of various sizes and colors: some with clouds and some with rings and others surrounded by dozens of moons.

"But our search was in vain," the voice went on. "For there was no planet to take the place of ours. We drifted through the galaxy for centuries, watching our people grow old and die. There were fewer children being born as time went by because our people began losing their will to go on. Why, they asked, should we condemn our young to spend their lives in a city of metal, drifting in a never-ending night? Without a world of grass and trees and sky and wind — what was the purpose of going on?

"We examined thousands of planets, but we were unable to breathe their air. We gave up all hope. And then we came upon this planet hidden away on the outskirts of our galaxy."

As she spoke, I was in space again, floating above the city-ship as it came up to a familiar planet. I recognized it immediately. It was blue and reddish brown, swirled with white clouds.

The female alien went on. "We found that this planet had everything our previous world had had: the right temperatures, gravity, soil, water, food — everything, that is, except an atmosphere we could breathe.

"We were weary of searching for the perfect world. Our people were patient — we've had to be — but seeing how much more beautiful your planet was than all the others brought us near madness. We were tired. We couldn't look any farther. We had to make Earth our home!

"The military overthrew our government while we debated what to do next. Then our generals struck upon a unique plan to save our race. Their idea was for us to live on Earth, but not in our bodies, since your air was poisonous to us. Their plan was to genetically transplant our brains into human bodies. That way we could live on your planet. Most of us were appalled at the idea. But what was the alternative? At least, our generals told us, this way our minds could go on. It would preserve the souls of our race; for, as our philosophers agreed, that is the essence of any civilization. The body is only a vessel that holds the mind and soul together. So, they reasoned, what difference does it make what that body looks like if it means continuing our civilization?

"We were desperate. And desperate people sometimes do desperate things.

"Our scientists began working on their plan."

In the dream state I was in, I saw a tiny sleek ship — what people have been calling flying saucers — shoot out of the city-ship floating in space above Earth. Then I spotted several more saucers fly away, all of them heading for Earth. I found myself aboard one of the saucers. Four alien soldiers were in the ship, one of them operating strange controls with his seven-fingered hands.

We landed in a field under cover of night. Two of the snake creatures got into what looked like a bobsled with a glass dome. It left the saucer and flew over the dark land, with my dream-body following behind it. The sled floated into a town of old brick buildings with dirt streets. Dim lights glowed on black iron lamp posts standing on street corners. A few Model T Fords were parked along the curbs, with some horses and buggies joining them. Several men walked along the sidewalks in clothes from the early 1900s. But the people didn't seem to notice the sled, and I knew the aliens were using their power to block their minds — although the horses whinnied nervously as we glided silently by them. The sled stopped by a young couple sitting on a park bench under a street light. The man was dressed in a World War I army uniform and the woman wore a long white dress. Both suddenly slumped over. Then the aliens loaded them in the sled and left.

The dream vision turned into what looked like a laboratory inside the city-ship. Alien scientists were bent over dozens of dead humans while others were doing things with human brains, all of this under the watchful eyes of the alien soldiers.

The female's voice returned inside my head to narrate the story.

"The plan was to extract a single brain cell from each of us on the city-ship and combine it with a human brain cell, both genetically engineered to grow a new brain: one that would function like that of a normal human until the time came for the change. Then we had to construct embryos from the human males and females we had brought on board so that our scientists could grow human bodies in our laboratories. The ultimate goal was to create a being with an adult human body: a body that could live on Earth but had the mind — the memory and soul — of us locked inside it. This way each of us on the city-ship could begin life anew with our cloned brains growing inside a human body. It was a tradeoff: keeping our brains, but living in a human shape. Our only desire was to settle in some remote part of your world, away from earthlings, to start a new life in our new bodies, and even hope that happiness would return to us once again.

"But we met one failure after another. The human embryos wouldn't develop in our laboratory. After years of fruitless attempts, we tried implanting the reconstructed embryos in Earth women — unsuspecting women — in the hope that the embryos would grow there. But these attempts continued to fail. Either the fetuses died or developed into genetic monsters. We worked on the problem for decades, and as we did, our hopes dwindled. Many of us wondered from the very beginning if it was worth trading bodies; for the human body is as loathsome to us as our bodies are to you. Our people took a vote. The majority of us demanded that we stop these experiments and continue searching for another planet. For our astronomers insisted that there had to be a sister planet somewhere in the galaxy. Somewhere among all those stars had to be a planet where we could live. But our generals were determined to have their way, and the experiments went on, until at last the military government was overthrown and our new leaders decided we must leave."

The dream picture changed again. I was on the edge of the dark side of our moon. A small Earth hovered in the far distance over the crest of white jagged mountains. The city-ship sat silently in dark shadows at the bottom of a deep crater. Then it lifted out of the crater and rose into the starry lunar sky and flew away from Earth.

I woke up in the barn.

The eight of us had been standing there, sharing the same dream, and we were blinking around at each other, amazed at what we'd seen. Sharon and I had been holding on to each other the whole time, and when she came out of the dream she wrapped her arms around me even tighter.

The two aliens standing before us seemed to be coming out of a trance themselves. They blinked and focused their large golden eyes back down on us.

Then David stammered, "You mean . . . this experiment we're in . . . this whole thing was —"

"It was a mistake," the female alien finished for him. "How can we tell you how sorry we are for what we've done to you? It was long ago, while your mothers were pregnant with you, that we decided these experiments were getting us nowhere. That's when our people left to continue searching for another world.

"We left behind a patrol ship to monitor the children we'd made in the slim hope that perhaps this last attempt would be successful, in case we couldn't find another planet to live on. But this experiment ended in failure like all the others. We were told by our monitoring ship that not only were your brains changing a year before they were supposed to, but that your bodies were changing, too — which, of course, wasn't supposed to happen. But we weren't surprised.

"It was unwise to leave your embryos behind on Earth. Many of our scientists wanted to retrieve them before we left, but our leaders insisted on this one last experiment, just in case we were successful.

"We hurried back as quickly as we could." Her eyes dropped to the floor. "We're so sorry this has happened to you. I hope all of you understand . . ." Her voice trailed off.

I stood there trying to digest it all. It was too much to take in at one time. Then I asked the one question that had me really confused. "But my body didn't change. How come?"

It was the male who answered. "It means that you are the closest our scientists have ever come to creating the kind of new being we were after." He hesitated. "And that also means that we must keep you secret from our people. If they knew how close they had come to being successful, they would return and continue the experiments. And that I must not allow to happen."

The female looked over at her companion and nodded in agreement.

He continued. "All the others in this experiment have been taken aboard our patrol ships to return to the city-ship. But your group must remain here. I cannot take you away from your planet. Not now."

Hearing those words made our spirits leap! We were staying! Before we could restrain ourselves, we burst out in a chorus of shouting and rejoicing and backslapping that amazed the aliens. But the male had more to say, so we calmed down and listened.

"I don't know how you changed your friends back to human form," he said to me. "Somehow, during the changing process, you developed a power we don't possess. All the more reason to keep this secret. When I go back, I'll tell my superiors that we didn't get here in time and that all of you suffocated while waiting for us. That I incinerated you, with no traces left behind." He thought for a moment, studying me. "The patrol ship made its report about you, but I think I can fix that problem, too.

I'll tell them you died of a brain malfunction, and that I eliminated you, also.

"Something — some kind of unforeseen genetic recombination — has affected your brain cells. It's a mystery to me. I don't know if your body will stay the way it is — or even your friends' bodies, as far as that goes." Then he said to all of us, "It might be that at some point in your lives the chemical triggering compound inside you could go off again, changing you all back into our form. Or it could be that what your friend here has done to you will prevent that from ever happening again. I simply don't know." He leveled his large eyes on me once more. "It could be that you will have to stay with your friends for the rest of their lives. You may have to be there to help them in case they do begin to change again. I hope that never happens. I hope you and your friends can go on with your lives just as though none of this ever happened. I know that will be difficult, but you must try. At least you have a beautiful world to live in. And for that you should be very grateful."

He started to say something more but didn't. A sadness came over his face. Then he concluded, "We must go. You were the last to be picked up and we're late in getting back. Goodbye. And good luck."

He turned and moved out of the barn on his giant rippling tail.

The female watched him go, then turned back to us and said, "Please. You must not judge us by what our people have done here. Survival is the most basic force in the universe. That is all we are trying to do — survive." She glanced back at the door. "His brother was one of the scientists working on this project. I don't think he'll ever get over the shame he feels. He wanted this assignment, to come here and take the children in the experiment away. It was his way of putting an end to this . . . this horrible mistake." She gave us a sad smile. "But I think that seeing all of you — seeing how you survived the experiment — has done him some good. At least he can look back and remember the one group of humans who escaped this ordeal. Maybe he'll be able to sleep a little easier now."

With that, she said, "Goodbye," and glided out of the barn.

I stood there, not knowing what to do or say. We all did.

Then Sharon gave me an urgent look. "Steve, it wasn't their fault," she said. Then she took us all in with a pleading voice. "Don't you see? It wasn't their fault!" She gripped my arm. "Steve, we can't just let them go like this. Someone has to tell them!"

No one said anything.

"Then I will!" She headed for the doorway.

"Wait!" I said. "We'll all go."

We ran out of the barn and came to an abrupt halt. Our eyes fell on their patrol ship. It was a flying saucer the size of a large house, sleek and beautiful, reflecting the growing light in the sky from its silvery body.

The two aliens were standing by the side of the ship

when a slit appeared in the smooth metal, opening into a door.

We walked up to them.

"Hold it," I said. "We want you to know something before you go."

The ten of us regarded each other for a silent moment.

"We forgive you," I said at last. The pair glanced at each other, then turned their golden eyes back on us.

"Thank you," the male said, and disappeared into the ship.

The female started to follow him, then turned to us and said, "But who will speak for the others in this experiment? And those in all the other experiments? How can the human part of them forgive us for what we did now that they are no longer human?"

None of us said anything as we watched her vanish behind a closing door that once again sealed into a smooth metal wall.

We stood back as the ship rose silently into the air, moving higher and higher, becoming smaller and smaller, until it blended in with the few stars left hanging in the twilight sky and disappeared into deep space.

# 21

# The End and the Beginning

We stood alone in the cool morning mist, staring up into the empty sky.

Somewhere a farm dog bayed in the distance, and from another direction a rooster crowed.

The first traces of light painted the eastern sky pink, and the land began taking on color as the farms and fields came into view, and all of us felt grateful to see another sunrise on our planet Earth.

"We made it." Sharon sighed. "Thank God we're still here." She glanced up into the bluing sky. "And not up there."

She held on to me and I held on to her; and in that moment we knew we had a lot of forgetting to do and a lot of planning ahead of us.

Scott spoke next. "Steve? Do you think there's a possibility that . . . we could start changing again . . . like they said?"

"I don't know, Scott. We're part of those creatures, and we're going to have to live with that for the rest of our lives. We'll never know what lasting effects their experiment will have on us."

Stephanie buried her face in David's chest. "I don't ever want to go through that again. Never!"

Terry looked over at me, attempting a grin. "Steve, I guess that means . . . we'll all have to stick with you for the rest of our lives, like they said. You suppose you could put up with us that long?"

I glanced around at the expectant faces of each person in the group, then joked back, "Wouldn't that fall under the category of cruel and unusual punishment?"

Jill smiled at each of us. "Now we have a reason to be with each other — always."

"All for one and one for all," Terry said. Then a thoughtful look crossed his face.

David walked up and stuck his hand out to me. "Thanks, Steve, for saving me. I don't even want to think of what would have happened if you hadn't —" And then, of all things, he hugged me. And if that wasn't bad enough, all the others hugged me, too, and I blushed right up to my ears.

Somewhere, a church bell rang out in the far distance, and we all remembered that it was Sunday morning.

"David!" Stephanie said. "I've got to get home! My parents still think I ran away!" She turned around to us. "Oh, no! What am I going to say? I can't tell them the truth!"

"Me, too," Roxann agreed. "What can any of us say? If we told them what happened, they'd haul us off in the nut wagon for sure."

Jill sounded worried. "Our parents are going to kill us for disappearing the way we did."

Scott answered, "At least we still have our parents to go home to. Anything they do will be a piece of cake compared to what almost happened to us."

"But," Jill said in a low, unsure voice, "they aren't

really our parents . . . are they? Not now."

"Oh yes they are," Sharon countered almost angrily. "They're more our parents now than they ever were before."

No one said anything for an awkward moment.

"Hey," I said, looking around at them. "Has anything really changed? Are we going to go back and act any differently toward our parents and blow it just because of a little genetic technicality? Come on, now. We're stronger than that, aren't we? No damn aliens are going to change our lives. Right?"

The others snapped out of their spell and nodded around in agreement. We were all in the same boat and, as always, we had to pull together to make it through this.

"Oh, no!" David said. "The police! We put them to sleep at that house on Chestnut! What are we going to tell them?"

Terry said, "If that's the biggest problem we have to face after all we've been through, then I'll take it — on a platter."

And that produced smiles all around.

We were quiet for a moment. Then David said, "It's like being reborn, isn't it? We've all been given a second chance."

Stephanie looked back into the early morning sky wistfully. "All those other kids in the experiment . . . The ones who didn't make it. I feel so sorry for them."

Which made us thoughtful all over again.

But this wasn't the time to stand around and sort out emotions.

"Hey," I said. "Let's get going. We've got homes to go back to. We've got worried families waiting for us. Come on."

But Sharon held up her hand. "Wait a second."

We halted and wondered what she wanted.

She looked at us, then at the hazy farmland stretched out all around, then over at some deer watching us in the distance as they stood shoulder deep in ground fog. Then she gazed up at the sky as the tip of the sun peeked up over a field of corn, then listened as the last bell from the church clanged over the peaceful country, then turned her shining eyes back on us.

"Okay," she said at last. "I'm ready. Let's go."

Four of us piled into Sharon's mother's car and four others got into Sergeant Coffee's car. We backed them out onto the deserted highway and headed home to Summerville.

And never looked back.